CRAVING REDEMPTION

FORBIDDEN SERIES #4

TRACY LORRAINE

Edited by Pinpoint Editing

Proofread by Paige Sawyer Proofreading

Cover design & formatting by Sammi Bee Designs

Andy and Amelia

A NOTE

Craving Redemption is written in British English and contains British spelling and grammar. This may appear incorrect to some readers when compared to US English books.

CHAPTER ONE

"YOU WANT THE USUAL?" I watch as Joe gestures for the barman. Much to everyone else's annoyance, she takes one look at him and saunters over, ignoring her other customers who have been waiting longer.

"What can I get you, handsome?" She bats her very fake eyelashes at him, and he leans forward on his elbows, eating the attention right up.

Rolling my eyes at them, I glance around the bar. It's not unusual to bump into a couple of the guys from work here. This place might be a little classier than it was back in the day, but it's still our regular. It was called Fire back then and was full of drunken students. Now, it's a fancy bar called The Avenue and has chrome fittings everywhere and chandeliers hanging from the high ceilings. I'd like to think we've also grown and are a little more sophisticated, but I usually end up questioning that once we get a few drinks inside us.

"Here you go," Joe sings, sliding a prosecco towards me. "To your awesome new housemate." He clinks his glass to mine, his face deadly serious.

"You're an idiot." I can't help but laugh at his puppy dog eyes.

I haven't lived with anyone since my ex suddenly vanished on me a little over six months ago. I must admit that I'm looking forward to having someone else to talk to. Joe promised me it would be only a short-term fix for his little homeless problem, but I'm in no rush to get rid of him—well, not yet, anyway. We've only been living together for a few days. I've not had the chance to discover if he has any weird quirks I'm not going to be able to deal with.

If I start finding stray toenails littered over the bathroom floor, there are going to be issues.

"So, anyone catch your attention?" I shake myself from my nightmare and look up into his dark eyes.

"Huh?"

"Anyone catch your eye?"

"Oh no, I'm not really interested." I've been going through somewhat of a dry spell recently. When I admitted how long it had been since I'd had sex, Joe immediately demanded I put on my sluttiest dress and dragged me out of the flat.

I was excited in the taxi on the way here but now, looking around and finding absolutely no one who catches my eye, I kind of want to go home, put my pyjamas on, and snuggle up on the sofa.

Joe's brow rises before he turns to scout the perfect man for me himself. I know it's unlike me. I used to have a reputation for being the party girl, but, after my last two bad experiences with men, I'm more than happy keeping my distance for a while.

Sipping my drink, I keep my focus on the colourful bottles behind the bar. I used to live for this, for a night out and the thrill of meeting someone new, but with everything that's happened over the past few months, I've totally lost the enthusiasm.

"Erica, come on. You need to get yourself back out there. Hiding isn't healthy. It's not *you*."

"Maybe it's the new me," I mutter, sipping my drink. "Anyway, who are you to start dishing out advice? I hate to break it to you, mate, but your life isn't all that great right now."

"What makes you say that?"

"Oh, come on. You can't tell me you don't realise you've been moping around since the day you moved out of yours and Lauren's flat. I know you miss her. I'm trying not to let it affect me, being your new roommate and all." I wink to let him know I'm only winding him up. If he needs time to 'grieve' or whatever the fuck it is he's doing, he's more than welcome to it. I know he appreciates my offer of a place to stay.

"I just—"

"You can say it, you know, that you miss her. I know how tight you two were."

"Yeah, fine. I miss her, okay?" Something passes through his eyes, and it only feeds my earlier suspicion that there might be more to this than he's letting on.

I open my mouth to say more, but I don't get the chance. Joe is too keen to change the subject.

"Do not tell me you passed up the guy at ten o'clock?"

Following his instruction, I look to my left and immediately lock eyes with a handsome older man. A shiver runs down my spine as our eye contact holds. I can't tell from this distance what colour they are, but they're dark. Ripping my gaze away, my mouth waters when I take in his pristine white shirt covered with a sharp black waistcoat. *Fuck.* I'm a sucker for a man in a suit.

"He is *so* your type, and by the way he's staring at you like he wants to devour you, I'd say you're his, too."

"Nope, not interested. I am off men for the foreseeable future."

"Fuck off. You don't really expect me to believe that, do you? You're Erica Wilde, this is what you do: go out, have fun, pick up guys." I wince at his opinion of me.

"Well, if that's how you see me, it's even more reason for me to swear off men."

"I didn't mean it like that, and you know it. I just meant that...fuck, I'm screwing this up. You're not yourself right now, and I hate it. You've lost that sparkle in your eye. Your zest for life. *He* stole that from you."

"No," I spit. "We do not talk about him. *Ever.* You got that?"

"I know. I'm just...I'm worried about you."

"I could say the same thing."

"I'm fine. I just need a good fuck. You've been winding me up all week, walking around in those little fucking shorts and practically see through top—"

"That top is not see through."

"Maybe not, but I sure as shit know you don't wear a bra under it."

"Yeah, you really do need a fuck." I pull my eyes from his and look around, much like he did for me earlier. "Guy or girl?"

"A guy. Definitely a guy. I need him to—"

"Spare me."

Rolling his eyes, he moves to scan the room, looking for his target.

With Joe's attention averted, I risk another look at the suit. My skin's been burning the entire time we were talking, so I know he hasn't got bored and moved on. Our eyes lock once again, and I swear they fucking call to me. They drop to my lips and I watch as his tongue sneaks out and runs along his bottom one. My thighs clench and my fingers curl around the bar stool I'm perched on as my body temperature spikes.

I allow myself a minute to appreciate him.

His eyes are hard, and there are a few lines creasing his forehead. His lips are pressed into a thin line. From anger or desire? Only he knows, but damn if I don't want to go over there and find out. He's got the perfect amount of stubble on his jaw, just enough to enhance what I'm sure his mouth is capable of but not enough to leave a rash.

Biting down on my bottom lip, I try to imagine what it might be like to be with a man who looks as dominant and dangerous as him. I've experienced my fair share of demanding lovers, but he looks like he might be capable of taking it to the next level. Tingles ignite in my core as I think about how capable he probably is.

"I'd put one hundred quid on you leaving with him tonight," Joe says in my ear. I laugh but my eyes don't leave the suit's for even a second.

"You don't have any money, and we both know it, so how about you keep the gambling to a minimum?"

"You just know you'll lose. If you need me, I'll be over there. Good luck."

I expect him to get up and walk off, but to my surprise, Joe grabs my chin, tilts my head back and slams his lips to mine. My eyes widen in shock, as do the suit's. "Knock him dead, sweets." And then he's off into the crowd, as if that just didn't happen.

Downing what's left of my drink, I fight to stop my lips curling up in satisfaction when I watch the suit rise from his seat. I quickly try to decide what I should do. Sadly, any decision I might have been coming to is taken away the moment a man slides onto the vacant stool beside me. The first thing I notice is his scent; it's expensive and sexy as fuck. My mouth waters, wondering how it might make his skin taste. Next is the heat of his breath as it skates over my neck, and then it's the deep timbre to his voice. It's so rough it has a slow throb erupting between my legs.

"See, I had him down as your gay best friend. But that wasn't the kiss of a gay man."

"And you would know that how?" My voice comes out as a breathy whisper, and I immediately chastise myself for being so swept away by him already.

"Because he knows how to kiss a woman."

"Did you come over here to discuss how my friend kisses?"

"No, I came to tell you that it worked."

"Huh?" I ask, turning to him for the first time. It's a stupid mistake, because what I thought was a seriously handsome man from across the bar I soon see is breathtakingly gorgeous—and terrifyingly dangerous close-up.

"You weren't listening to him, so he took matters into his own hands. And here I am."

"Yeah...here you are."

His low chuckle causes my temperature to kick up a few more notches. "We'll have a bottle of whatever she's drinking, and I'll have another." He pushes his tumbler towards the barmaid who's looking at him much like she was Joe earlier. *Hussy.* She takes a few moments to appreciate the masculine beauty in front of her before turning to fulfil his order. When he turns back, his eyes narrow in confusion. "What?"

"Oh nothing, Casanova."

His lips curl in an amused smirk. "Oh, her." Shifting forward on his stool, his legs surround mine and my breath catches the second we connect. "There's only one woman I can see in this bar, sweetheart." His hand reaches out and gently tucks a lock of my curled red hair behind my ear. Naturally I'm a mousey brunette, but after my last disaster I decided a change was needed so I went for the brightest box money could buy.

Our eyes hold, and suddenly everything around me disappears. It's just me and him, the captivating darkness of his eyes, and the sizzle of electricity that sparks between where our legs are touching.

"Thank you." Reaching out for the glass the barmaid pushes my way, I rip my eyes from his and take a very large sip of the small amount she poured. It's not enough, but I fear the bottle might not be, either.

CHAPTER TWO

"DANCE WITH ME," he demands after a few seconds of heavy silence between us. His hand reaches out, his fingers twisting with mine. It's the first time I've been able to appreciate his muscular, tattooed forearms that are showcased by his rolled-up sleeves.

"I'm not sure that's a good idea."

"It's not optional."

"But...my drink." It's my last attempt to put off the inevitable. The tension between us crackled while we were just sitting here. I can only imagine what it's going to be like once my body's moving to the music alongside his.

A little of the 'old' me trickles through my veins.

So what I've been screwed over by the previous men I've allowed between my legs? That shouldn't stop me from enjoying myself, especially when it's with someone who looks like the man currently pulling me from my bar stool, offering me a release I so desperately need.

He catches the barmaid's attention, and her eyes light up when she realises who's calling before he barks, "Put it on ice. We'll be back."

She nods and he takes off across the bar. While this floor might be sophisticated these days, both up and downstairs are still clubs with dancefloors to die for. I usually go up, force of habit from my younger days, but when Suit gets to the stairs, he pulls me down. There's something about heading towards the basement with him that has excitement pulling at my lower stomach.

Maybe he's just what I need to drag me out of my rut and to re-start my life once again. Hell knows I've been spending too much time working—not that I really have a choice after the colossal mistakes I made that nearly forced the doors to close on the business for good. I push that thought to the back of my mind. I don't need to be worrying about that right now. I don't need to be worrying about *anything*.

As we descend, the beat of the bass starts to vibrate the floors and rumble through my feet. My heart begins to race and my muscles ache to be dancing, to feel his hot body up against mine and his hands roaming over my skin.

I've no clue what the song is; I'm too lost to the anticipation of what's to come next. In only a couple of minutes, he's shown me that he's a man who likes to be in control. I can't wait to find out how he dances, how he handles my body.

It's only a couple more seconds before I get to find out. His footsteps slow and his arm tugs until I'm forced to come up against his chest. With my favourite heels on, I'm not all that much shorter than him and I'm able to look up into his intense eyes. I'm just about able to see the silver flecks within the dark steel grey that give away his excitement.

The knowledge that he's feeling the same connection between us right now that I am has my stomach clenching in need. Suddenly, I wish we weren't in the middle of the dance floor, surrounded by other people. With his scent filling my nose, his dark stare filling my mind and his body pressed up against mine, the only thing I can think of is getting him out of his fancy suit and finding out exactly what he's hiding beneath.

The arm he's holding around my waist, keeping us locked together, tightens, and his hips roll in time with the music.

Holy shit, he can move.

Sliding my hands up his chest, the softness of the expensive fabric of his waistcoat caressing my palms, I wrap them around his neck and allow my fingers to tease the short hair at the nape.

His eyes drop from mine in favour of my lips, and I'm powerless to stop my tongue darting out in preparation for what I hope is to come.

The hand that isn't holding me threads in my hair. He grips with an almost painful force before his lips find mine.

The moment we connect, my body is on fire. My heart thunders in my chest, ensuring I can feel it in every part of my body. My skin tingles and my core aches. If he can dance and kiss like this, then I really want to find out what else he's capable of.

His tongue forces its way into my mouth and caresses against mine. My knees almost give out as this man takes over my body completely.

Nothing else exists. It's just the two of us, our bodies doing what they were designed to.

Our kiss continues, our tongues duelling as we fight to discover every inch of each other's mouths. Dropping his hand from my hair, he ghosts his fingers down my exposed spine. He swallows my moan, but not before I feel him hardening against my stomach.

Long before I'm ready, he rips his lips from mine and spins me around. My skin burns as he takes in my bare back before his hands land on my hips and my arse is pulled to him. One hand skates up my stomach and comes to rest on my ribs, dangerously close to my breast that's begging for his touch. My nipples are hard as bullets, the fabric of my dress brushing against them only adding to the pleasure building within me.

His lips kiss a trail down my neck. He sucks and bites, making me crazy with desire.

"You'd let me fuck you right here, wouldn't you?" The deep rumble of his voice only makes the answer to his question more obvious.

When my only response is to groan, he continues. "I wouldn't, because I'd have to kill every motherfucker who laid eyes on you."

Jesus.

"But that doesn't mean I don't want to."

Resting my head back against his shoulder, I look up to his hooded eyes. "Take me home."

His eyes get even darker, and the hint of danger in them has heat pooling between my legs. It's been too long, and I need what he's offering more than I need my next breath.

"Let's go." His voice, deep, rough and powerful, vibrates through me. The second his hot palm lands on my lower back, I follow his lead, away from the dance floor and up the stairs.

"I thought we...oh." He pushes me in the direction of the bar. I watch in delight as he leans over and shows off his round arse as he grabs the bottle waiting for me.

"We might need this." His expression is neutral. Anyone around us wouldn't register what I know he's thinking about, but I see it in his eyes. I might have only known him for a few short minutes in reality, but I see it: the desire behind the mask.

With his fingers wrapped around the bottle and his other hand burning the small of my back, he guides me to the exit.

I expect to head towards an awaiting taxi, so I'm surprised when he pushes me a little farther down the street and stops beside a gun metal grey Jaguar.

I miss his contact the moment he pulls his hand away and reaches for the door. Pulling it open, he looks down at me. His face is hard, his lips pressed into a thin line, but his eyes are still burning with fire.

"Thank you."

No sooner has my arse hit the leather seat than he slams the door shut and I watch as he makes his way around the bonnet towards the driver's door.

"Should you be driving?" I ask, realising that I've no idea how much he's had to drink.

"Do you trust me?"

I consider my answer for a moment. His stare

turns to me; he's obviously waiting for my answer before committing to this.

I could lie, but that's not really my style, so instead I go with the truth and hope like hell it won't put an end to this. "No. Quite honestly, I don't trust anyone but myself."

"Good answer."

His foot presses down on the accelerator and the roar of the engine vibrates through me. My thighs clench and my nails dig into the leather beneath me.

"Fuck."

I'm jolted back in my seat as the car lurches forward and sets off on a race through the city.

It's only a few short minutes before the car screeches to a halt in a part of town I know well.

"You live here?"

"Yeah, temporarily. Problem?"

"No, not at all. Lead the way."

With his hand possessively placed on the small of my back once again, he guides me through the entrance of the building and towards the lift.

Silently, he presses the button for the top floor and then turns on me. Taking a step back, I bump into the handrail and wobble on my heels a little. I've only had one drink, but I think him on top of that is enough to catch me off-guard.

His steel eyes drop from mine in favour of my

body. My temperature rises under his stare and my heart starts to race. Tingles follow his eyes as they travel around my body, and my muscles ache to reach out for him, needing to feel his skin against mine.

The second he does step towards me, it's like the air has been pulled from the enclosed space. His scent gets stronger and my mouth waters to find out how he might taste.

His forearms cage me in as he continues staring down at me. His eyes bounce between mine and I start to wonder if he can read something in them or if he's trying to figure something out. Either way, I'm not sure I like it. I don't need anyone trying to make sense of the shit in my head. What I really need is for someone to take it away, to allow me to forget all my fuck-ups and bad decisions. I'm pretty sure he's very capable of that if he would just step into action.

When the elevator doors open, signalling our arrival, he steps away once again, rests his hand where it seems to be quite at home on my lower back, and guides me towards an oak door.

I expect to find a bachelor pad behind it. This man screams 'minimalistic' with black and chrome everywhere, so I'm a little surprised when the door's pushed open and I discover a very plain, nondescript flat.

Deciding not to focus on how he lives, I run my

hand down his arm and turn into his body. "Which way's your bedroom?"

The muscles in his neck ripple as he swallows, making me desperate to run my tongue along them.

"Down the hall, last room on the left. I'll get glasses," he says, holding up the bottle of prosecco that's still in his hand.

Turning so I'm walking backwards, I take in his body: the perfect fit of his white shirt stretching over his strong arms, and the open collar, sans tie, that allows just a hint of the tattoos hiding beneath, the crisp cut of the waistcoat and the slim dark trousers that clearly show off his excitement.

He watches me until I'm forced to turn around and see where I'm actually going. Finding the door, I push it open and slip inside. Like every other room in this flat, it's cream with wooden furniture, not really all that exciting, and nothing like the man himself.

Spotting a door at the other end of the wall, I hope to find an en suite to freshen up in. I make quick work of my business before throwing my hair over my head to give it a little more volume and reapplying my gloss.

I expect him to be waiting for me once I leave the confines of his bathroom, but I'm disappointed to find the bedroom still empty.

The lights of the city beyond call to me, and I walk over to the huge window and stare out at the night sky and the lights in all the buildings beyond. We're just high enough to be able to see over the building opposite and, without it in the way, there's an incredible view.

My heart continues its steady beat as the anticipation grows within me. He's here somewhere —I can hear him, but why is he not in here with me? There's no way he's regretting this. He was as on board as I am when we arrived.

Worrying my necklace, I wonder if maybe he's waiting for me to find him. Deciding to take matters into my own hands, I turn but don't get a chance to take a step, because he's there, standing in the doorway, filling the space with his solid frame. My mouth goes dry and I fight to swallow. His waistcoat is gone and his shirt's unbuttoned, giving me an even better view of the hard lines of his muscles and the intricate patterns of his ink.

He steps into the room and places the bottle and two glasses onto a dresser before returning his attention to me.

"Come here," he demands.

My feet move of their own accord until I'm standing inches from his body. His heat seeps into me and moisture floods my mouth once again. I swallow it and lick my lips as my eyes flit down to his. I need to feel them on me once again.

My nipples pebble against the fabric of my dress, and the lace between my legs gets wetter the longer he stares down at me.

"You get one warning." A shiver runs down my spine at his deep, scratchy voice. "I tell you what to do, you do it. Got that?"

Holy shit. My knees tremble with need for this man to do exactly what he wants to me. I hoped he'd be dominant and demanding, and, so far, he's excelling my expectations.

"I need you to trust me not to take it too far. This is about pleasure, not pain." He winks, and my stomach lurches. "But if you need to stop, say..." He pauses as he thinks of a word.

"Pineapple."

"Pineapple?" His brows pull together in amusement, and I shrug. "What's your name?" I ask, suddenly realising that the only thing I know about this man is where he lives. "I need to know what to scream when you make me come."

"When I *allow* you to come, you can call me anything you like, sweetheart."

"Huh." I would have put money on him requesting me to call him Sir...or even Daddy.

"Anything else?" Something sparkles in his eyes,

I'm not sure if it's amusement or frustration that we've barely started and I'm already not doing what I'm told.

"Um...no, I think I'm good."

"You think?"

I take a small step towards him and run my fingertips down the skin his open shirt exposes. He doesn't react apart from the ripple of his abs when I get to them.

I flinch when his warm fingers brush my shoulders, pulling my spaghetti straps down and allowing the fabric of my loose-fitting dress to flutter down my body and pool at my feet. I gasp when the cool air surrounds my breasts and my nipples tighten, begging for attention.

Taking a step back, his eyes drop and he bites down on his bottom lip as he takes his time assessing what I've got to offer. My insecurities threaten to make themselves known, but I fight them down. I desperately want to say something sarcastic, but his earlier dominant tone stops me. I don't think he'd be amused right now.

"Get on your knees."

My eyes fly up to his, shocked by his bluntness but not the least bit turned off. How I'm feeling right now is very much the opposite.

Following his instructions, I drop to the floor and

immediately reach for the waistband of his trousers. I can already see his cock straining against the fabric and, in my haste to unveil it, I fumble about with the button.

His eyes burn into the top of my head. I can feel his frustration levels growing the longer this takes me, but at no point does he help me out. I'm not usually this much of a klutz, but there's something about his steel eyes and dominance that has me off-kilter.

Eventually the fabric parts, and I'm able to push both his trousers and boxers down his muscular thighs. His cock springs free and my eyes widen before flying up to his.

Usually I'm irritated by the arrogant smirk that plays on a guy's lips, but team

it with his intense eyes and it only makes me want him more.

His eyebrow lifts and I remember that I was doing something before I got lost in his dark stare.

Looking back down to his cock, I lick my lips, take it in my hand and run my tongue around the head. A loud groan filters down from him. It's all the encouragement I need.

Licking down his shaft, I revel in the feeling of it twitching under my touch. Smiling, I pull back and watch as my tiny hand wraps around his width and pumps him a few times before leaning forward once again and taking him in my mouth.

"Fuck," he grunts above me, and I push him deeper until he hits the back of my throat. His fingers twist in my hair, his grip painful but not unwelcome as I continue working him.

Dragging my nails down his stomach and thighs results in his pre-come coating my tongue. Lapping at the head, I take everything he's got.

He's getting close when I'm forcefully pushed back and then pulled to my feet. His lips slam down on mine, one hand gripping the hair at the back of my head and the other on my arse as he walks me backwards. His hard body presses against my curves, making me desperate to feel us skin to skin. Reaching up, I push the cotton from his shoulders so I can run my palms over his bare upper arms.

We must reach the bed, because suddenly I'm released and pushed backwards. My arse bounces on the edge and he reaches for my knickers, ripping them from my body before he finishes the job I started with his clothing and pulls his shirt from his arms and his trousers and boxers from his legs.

My eyes feast on the inches upon inches of toned skin before me. If it wasn't already abundantly clear with his clothes on, then it is now: this man works out, and works out a lot.

I'm in pretty good shape, but I'm by no means a gym bunny, and I suddenly feel a little less confident about my body. It only lasts a few seconds because he wraps his hands around my thighs, pushing them wide and forcing me to lie back as he drops to his knees. Needing to witness what he's about to do, I prop myself up on my elbows and stare down as he lowers himself to my centre.

He blows out a stream of hot breath that has my hips lifting from the bed and my fingers gripping the sheets beneath me.

His low chuckle has more desire pooling at my entrance. He hovers less than an inch away from me and I can already feel my anticipation building. It's been quite a long time since I saw a man's head between my legs, and even longer since one looked quite as fucking good as he does right now.

I'm just at the point of voicing my frustration when he moves forward, parts me further and sucks my clit into his hot mouth.

"Argh," I cry out as every muscle in my body pulls tight with pleasure. He continues sucking, my back arching off the bed in my need for more, then he presses his tongue down on my clit and it's like my entire body sighs with relief. This has been a long time coming, and it grows faster than I've ever known.

He eats me like no man ever has before. He oozes confidence with his considered movements and teases to the perfect spots. The feeling of him stretching me open with two of his fingers is almost enough to push me over the edge, but just as I think I'm going to fall he stops all movement. My core clenches are nothing as my entire body aches and mourns the pleasure I was right on the brink of.

"Jesus, fuck."

His eyes flit up to mine and I swear they're fucking smiling while my chest heaves and I fight to demand he continue. It would be pointless; it's abundantly clear that only one person's demands are to be heard in this room, and they sure as fuck aren't mine.

Sitting back, a smile tugs at his lips. I don't know what I expected; he's already warned me about *letting* me come.

Starting at my thigh, his lips trail up my body as he crawls on top of me. He licks a line up the centre of my stomach before stopping to suck each of my nipples into his mouth, electric sparks shoot straight to my core, keeping my release just within touching distance. My fingers tangle in his hair in an attempt to keep him there, knowing that if he continues long enough it'll be enough to push me over the edge.

When his fingers find my pussy once again, I

start to believe he's going to allow me to come, but, just like before, he has me right on the edge before he pulls his fingers out and his hot mouth away from my body.

"You're a fucking tease," I manage between my laboured breaths.

"Don't pretend you don't fucking love it." Lifting his fingers, I expect him to bring them to his mouth, but instead he runs one along my bottom lip. "Open." I do as I'm told, and he slides the two fingers that were just deep inside me into my mouth.

His eyes flash with desire as I close my lips and wrap my tongue around them. The silver I spotted earlier is almost like diamonds as he stares down at me like he's about to devour me.

"Fuck."

One second I'm sucking on his fingers, and the next his lips are on mine in an all-consuming kiss, his body pressing mine into the mattress. My hands lift from the bed and I find the hot, smooth skin of his back. Dragging my nails down, a moan rumbles up his throat, but I swallow any noise that might have erupted.

He moves so he's back between my legs, his cock nudging at my entrance. I push up, trying to find what I so desperately need, but one large hand on my hip stops any further movement.

"When I say," he repeats, his eyes not leaving any room for argument.

He continues rubbing himself against me, driving me fucking crazy with need before folding himself over my body, his breath tickling my ear when he comes to a stop.

"Unless you stop me right now...I'm taking you bare. I'm clean, I swear."

"Oh fuck," I moan, my imagination running wild with how his thick length will feel, stretching me open and filling me completely.

CHAPTER THREE

MY BACK ARCHES, my nails scratching across his shoulders as he thrusts inside me. My muscles clench as my body tries to accept his size after being ignored for so long.

"So fucking good," he groans into my neck.

He thrusts his hips slowly a couple of times, like he knows I need a moment, before he sits up, slides his hands under my arse and lifts me just so. I squeal as he hits me in the perfect position, my nails digging into the skin of his thighs. My breasts bounce, my skin flushing as he slams into me, over and over. His grip on me is bruising, and I know I'll have his fingertips marked on my skin for days, reminding me of this. Coming here with him might be irresponsible, irrational, but right this second it's the best decision I've made in a long fucking time.

"Oh god. Fuck. So good."

"Eyes," he barks when mine flicker closed. They immediately fly open at his demand and lock onto his. "You going to come around my cock?"

"Yes, yes," I chant as he continues to pound into me. "Please." My voice is almost begging. It's so close I can almost taste it, but I fear I might not be allowed it yet—and I'm right, because just as the beginning of my release tingles in my lower stomach, he pulls out of me and flips me over.

With my arse in the air and my face smashed against his pillow, he lines up and thrusts back into me. I cry out, this angle and his length almost too much to bear, but he doesn't let up as he fucks me into next week.

"You on birth control?" His voice is low and deep, and I barely hear it.

"Yes."

One of his hands fists my hair, keeping my head low, and the other continues to grip my hip painfully hard, my arse slapping against him with every thrust until he releases my hip right before I'm about to crash over the edge. My orgasm hits at the exact same time his palm slaps down on my arse cheek. The sound of the slap can only just be heard over my cry as my release completely takes over my body. I swear I black out for a few seconds, and when I come back around it's just in time to hear his growl of pleasure fill the room and feel his cock swelling inside me as he fills my pussy with everything he has.

"Fuck," he heaves, pulling out of me and falling to my side.

Sitting myself on the edge of the bed, I slip my shoes off and prepare to stand and find my discarded clothing. Once I'm confident my knees will hold me, I begin to wobble my way towards the bathroom, the semen he filled me with starting to run down my thighs.

"Grab the bottle on your way back."

Looking over my shoulder, I watch as he rolls onto his back and throws one arm over his eyes, his entire body on full display without a care in the world—but to be fair, if I were sculpted like that, I'd probably be more than willing to show it off as well.

I run my eyes down his chest and come to a stop on his cock. Even half-mast it's impressive. A deep ache inside me makes itself known, but we've had our fun. It's time for me to get the hell out and get home before Joe sends out a search party.

I do the best job I can of making myself look slightly respectable, but my cheeks are still flushed, and my green eyes are bright with desire.

I can still feel him inside me as I reach for the

door handle and go to step out. The second I cross the threshold, his eyes are on me. I scoop up my ruined knickers when I find them, followed by my dress.

"What the hell are you doing?" he barks when I go to pull my dress up my legs.

"Getting dressed?" It's not meant to come out as a question, but my voice rises when I get a look at his hard expression.

"I don't fucking think so. Get the bottle and get over here." I look between him and where I've got my dress halfway up as I try to decide what to do. Go home alone or get a little more of what he's got to offer? I'm not sure there's really anything to consider.

Dropping the fabric, I step out, grab the bottle and the glasses from the side as requested, and make my way back to the bed.

"Good girl."

"I'm not a fucking girl."

"Oh, sweetheart. I'm well aware."

I'm lifted and positioned across his waist, his now fully hard cock teasingly lining up with my pussy. Taking the glasses from my hand, he holds them out so I can fill them up.

CRACKING MY EYES OPEN, I try to remember where I am. When the weight of an arm resting over my waist takes my attention, things start falling into place.

The suit with the intense steel eyes.

My thighs clench as I remember all the things that happened in this room last night. Without even moving, I can tell that my insides are tender after weeks of neglect.

Managing to slide to the edge of the bed, I blink a couple of times at the bright light of the alarm clock. Five am. Fuck.

Gently lifting his arm, I slip out of bed, praying that he won't wake up. The last thing I need is the awkward morning after the night before. It's best I just get the hell out of here.

I rush to pull my dress on before swiping my bag and shoes from the floor and tiptoeing from his bedroom. His door squeaks a little as I pull it open, but when I look back, he's still out like a light. I desperately want to stand for a minute or two and appreciate the beauty of the sleeping man before me, but my fear of him waking up is enough to have me running.

In no time, I'm sliding the key into the lock of my own front door. My brain is still sleep and sex fogged, and the last thing I'm expecting is to find Joe racing towards the door looking panicked as I step inside.

"Jesus, Erica," he says, pulling me into his body.

"What's wrong?"

"You disappeared. I had no idea where you were, and you weren't answering your phone." His concern isn't something I'm used to, and I'm not sure how I feel about it.

"Sorry, I guess I'm just used to living alone and not answering to anyone."

He pulls back, his brows pinched together. "You don't have to answer to me. I just wanted to know you were safe. But now I know you are, I'm expecting to hear all the details. Please tell me you've been with the man with the waistcoat." His hand slips into mine and pulls me towards the kitchen. Depositing me on a stool, he turns and kickstarts the coffee machine. I desperately want to fall face-first into my bed and get some more sleep, but coffee is a strong second.

"Yeah, I left with him."

"And?" Joe turns and pins with hard a stare.

"And it was a great night."

"Do you want to tell your face?"

"I'm serious, it was a great night. He was...full on." Joe's eyes light up and his eyebrows wiggle.

"Keep going."

"He was just...I don't know. Intense."

"Intense is good. Memorable."

"Yeah, I guess."

Silence descends around us. Joe brings over two mugs and pours some milk into mine. He waits for me to take a sip before asking his next question. "You didn't want to leave him, did you?" My eyes fly to his, and I try to figure out how to best answer, but it seems I don't need to. "Oh my god. You like him."

"I've not had enough sleep for this," I moan.

"Are you going to see him again?"

"I doubt it. I just left him asleep in his bed. I don't even know his name."

"Fuck, that's hot. I need to find me one of those. It's been way too long."

"You didn't get lucky last night?"

"Nah, the best I got was a hand job while listening to our new neighbours going at it like fucking animals."

"TMI, Joe. TMI." He chuckles, leaning back against the counter.

"Just be glad you weren't here. You'd have been begging for it."

"Been there, done that, got the t-shirt." I run my eyes up and down his body, trying to look disgusted, but he just laughs at me.

"Shut the fuck up, you loved it."

I shrug, because there's no point denying it. The few times we've fooled around have been pretty great, especially for a guy who thinks he'll end up spending his life with a man. Who am I to argue? We were both single, and an orgasm is an orgasm at the end of the day.

"I'm going back to bed," I say, tipping away the dregs of my coffee and placing my mug in the sink.

"Right behind you, sweets."

I turn left into my room while Joe goes right. Shutting the door behind me, I lean back on it and a smile twitches at my lips. It's been quite a long time since someone stayed up worrying about me. It might make me feel a little weird, but at the same time it's nice knowing that someone cares enough.

Stripping out of my dress once again, I stand in front of the mirror in my en suite and assess the damage. It looks like a bird's nesting in my hair, my face is covered in smeared black make up, and my lips are swollen from the suit's kiss. Fuck only knows how Joe could take looking at me seriously. I look like a hot mess, but memories of how I ended up this way has desire tugging at my lower stomach. Did I do the right thing, leaving like that?

That single thought haunts me as I wash his scent from my body and lie in bed, waiting for sleep to claim me. I fear that the answer might be that it wasn't.

CHAPTER FOUR

BEFORE I KNOW IT, the weekend's over and I'm making my way down the street toward the tube station for my morning commute to work.

I've worked the same job since I dropped out of university when I was twenty. I never intended to stay, but I soon found myself at home in the small, family-run building company, and the time never really came that I wanted something else.

Lauren, the boss' daughter and our in-house accountant, soon became one of my best friends, and I loved spending my days sitting beside her as we worked. The younger guys on the firm were pretty awesome too, especially the one I now live with.

The fact that I still have the job is nothing short of a miracle after the monumental fuck-up I made. Everyone can tell me that it wasn't my fault, that I was manipulated, but that doesn't help me see it any better. As far as I'm concerned, I allowed it to happen. I allowed the boss, my best friend's dad, to manipulate his way into my bed and blackmail me into keeping his dirty, money laundering secrets. The way I see it, I'm just as guilty as he was. I may not have had a hand in any of the dodgy deals going on, but I sure helped keep his tracks hidden, and at the first threat to my job and my home I opened my legs for him almost willingly.

My cheeks heat as I remember those few months of my life. I'm pretty sure I'll forever be ashamed of myself, but I was at my wits' end, up to my eyeballs in debt thanks to my ex, and I needed help. I just didn't expect it to come with so many strings and so much betrayal.

"Morning," I sing, walking into the office, dropping my bag on my desk and heading straight for the coffee machine and kettle. I'm used to being the first in, but since the boss' heart attack and death a few weeks ago, his stepson and the rightful boss of this place returned and kicked everything into touch.

"Good weekend?" Ben asks, leaning his hip against the doorframe, watching me make both of us our first caffeine hit of the day.

"Yeah, not bad."

"The rings around your eyes tell a different story, E."

"How about yours? Things still good with Lauren?" I wave him off, not wanting to talk about what—or who—has kept my sleep at bay the last few nights. His whole face lights up at the mere mention of her name, and my stomach clenches. How hard is it to find someone who'll look like that when they hear my name?

"She's good. We spent the weekend redecorating Mum's bedroom so we could move into it."

Ben and Lauren have one hell of a story attached to their relationship, but after being apart for six years, they eventually managed to stop arguing for long enough to figure their shit out and embark on their second chance. I'm happy for them...as well as jealous as fuck.

"I can't believe your mum moved out just like that."

"You and me both. But hey, we've got the whole house to ourselves now." He winks at me, his eyes darkening, probably with some filthy memory I don't need the details of.

"I know I've said it before but I'm so glad you two sorted your shit out."

"Me too. Now it's your turn to find yourself a decent bloke."

"Ha, no. I don't think I'm destined for that."

"You never know. The man of your dreams might just walk through that door at any moment."

We both turn to look at the entrance to the office as the door opens right on cue. Unfortunately for me, it's just Lauren who walks in.

"Everything okay?" she asks when she realises we're both staring right at her.

I hate that I can see disappointment in her eyes every time she looks at me now. She says she understands everything that happened with her dad, and that she doesn't blame me for any of it, but it still hurts. I'll do anything to get our friendship back where it was.

"Just talking about Erica having a man."

"Erica's got a man?" Lauren asks, rushing over to get the gossip.

"Erica is standing right here. And no, I don't have a man nor do I need one. I've got Joe to babysit, that's enough for me right now."

"Babysit?" booms through the office, seconds before he also appears. "Since when did I need babysitting?"

"You've no idea," Lauren mutters, and the two of us laugh, both knowing what it's like to live with him.

"Did Erica tell you about the hot man she spent Saturday night with?"

"No, she was actually saying exactly the opposite."

"Just because I don't *have* a man doesn't mean I don't *make use* of one."

"Christ. I don't need to hear this on a Monday morning," Ben moans, grabbing his now full mug and walking away. "Feel free to do some work when you've all finished gossiping."

"Sure thing, boss," Lauren says with a laugh, saluting him, but he's already rounded the corner into his office. "So..." Her eyes turn back to me. "Tell me all about this man."

"Nothing to tell. Met him at The Avenue, he took me home, we fucked all night, I left."

"Wow, how romantic."

"Who said anything about romance?" She shrugs and I use her moment of silence to run to the safety of my desk. That doesn't mean I don't hear Joe filling her in with all the details of my conquest.

Shaking my head at the two of them, I turn my computer on and get ready to start a new week.

We've got a long few days ahead of us as we continue to fight to keep the business from going under after all of Lauren's dad's questionable investments and embezzlements, but it's also our last week in this building. This has been the home of Johnson & Sons for years, and I know Ben's feeling a little emotional about his decision to move the office to the garages at his family home. It's the right decision. It'll free up some much needed money, but we've got a lot of stuff to pack up and move. On top of that, we've got employees leaving who are concerned about the company's future, along with a new contracts manager starting.

"Erica, make sure you've got everything ready, Trey said he'd be here at ten. I want to at least try to look like we know what we're doing," Ben shouts from his office.

"We do know what we're doing."

"Speak for yourself." He's right. He's been gone for the last six years, so he's not exactly up to scratch with how things work around here these days. I've got every confidence in him fixing all the mistakes I allowed to happen and keeping the company going.

I'm bent over, stacking some of our files into a box ready to move, when a silence falls over the office. I dust my hands off on my skirt and turn around to see what's distracted everyone.

My chin drops and my hands start to tremble when I stare at the man standing in the doorway, waiting for someone to greet him. But it's not just any man. It's him, *the suit.* Only he's dressed more casually in a pair of dark jeans and a perfectly pressed white shirt. It's unbuttoned enough to remind me of how his skin tasted on my tongue, and his sleeves are rolled up to reveal the ink wrapping around them.

His steel eyes hold mine as tension crackles between us.

My heart races as I try to get my brain and body on the same page. Why's he here? I didn't even give him my name let alone my...fuck. Please tell me he's not—

"Trey, good to see you again," Ben booms from behind me, breaking the spell he'd cast over the office. I know that Lauren and Betty are staring at me; their eyes are burning into my skin.

My body is frozen as Ben walks over and the two men shake hands. He turns back, his eyes first finding Lauren's, but he soon notices that something's not right. His eyes narrow on me before Lauren attempts to help me out.

"Trey, it's so good to meet you at last." She marches over and accepts his hand when he holds it out for her. "We're excited to have you on board."

"Thank you. I'm looking forward to getting my feet under the table." My stomach twists and I almost double over when his eyes meet mine over her shoulder.

"Would you like a drink before we get started?"

"Black coffee would be great."

"Fantastic." Turning, Lauren pins me with a stare and starts walking towards me. When she's in reaching distance, she grabs my forearm and pulls me along with her.

"You fucked him, didn't you?"

"Wow, you don't beat around the bush."

"No time for bush beating. Is this going to be a problem because—" Terrified of what her next words could be, I cut her off.

"No, no problem. I just didn't think I'd ever see him again."

"Jesus, Erica. Is there anyone in this office you haven't slept with?" Her face twists, and I know she regrets the words the second they fall from her lips. "Shit, I didn't mean—"

"It's fine. And for the record, I've never slept with Ben."

"You'll never know how grateful I am for that." She tries to say it light-heartedly, but I hear the pain in her voice. I hurt her more than she'll admit by getting involved with her dad.

"I can't believe this is happening." Covering my face with my hands, I will the images that are on repeat in my head from Saturday night away. The last thing I need to picture when I go out there and look in his eyes is him thrusting into me from behind.

Fuck. My. Life.

I'm meant to be trying to redeem myself after everything, not just bouncing from one disastrous office hook-up to another.

"What am I meant to do?" I don't mean for the question to be out loud, but when Lauren turns to me, I realise it was.

"You square your shoulders, hold your head up high and walk out there like you own the place. Forget about where his fingers have been and what he looks like without his clothes on—"

"Not that easy," I mutter, making her chuckle.

"You're going to have to. He's here to help sort this place out, not spend his days trying to figure out the best way to get you to spread your legs again." I hear her warning loud and clear. *Do not sleep with another employee and fuck this up for all of us.*

Nodding at her, accepting that my mistake with her dad is going to haunt me for the rest of my life, I quickly head towards the toilets to freshen up before walking out there like she just suggested.

Blowing out a breath, I grab the mug of coffee Lauren made for him. It sloshes about a little as my hand trembles. I pick up the documents from my desk that I'd prepared for him and take everything into the office where he's chatting with Ben.

"Here you go," I say, handing over the mug, hoping that my voice comes out as strong as I intend.

His eyes meet mine and it's like someone knocks the wind out of me. Swallowing my desire, I place my folder on the table and consider how the hell I'm meant to have a serious conversation with him.

"I've got a few documents for you to fill in and sign, then I need to take copies of your ID and your qualifications."

"I'll leave you two to it. If you need anything before you start next week, just pick up the phone, yeah?" Ben says to Trey before nodding his head at both of us and leaving the room, taking all the air with him.

"I shouldn't keep you long."

"That's a shame, because I've got all day." The deepness of his voice has goosebumps pricking my skin.

"Well, I'm kind of busy, so if we could just focus on the task in hand that would be awesome."

"Sure thing, *sweetheart*."

"No," I snap. His body stills in surprise. "I'm not having any of..." I wave my hand in front of him. "That. We're colleagues now, apparently, so it's best we both forget everything that happened and move on. This job is important to me, and I won't have another mistake ruin it."

"Mistake, huh?" His eyes darken, as if he's remembering every second of our time together.

"Yes. *Mistake.* Can you fill this in, please?" I shove the personal details form at him and blow out a frustrated breath.

"Careful, I'll start to think you want to get rid of me."

I purse my lips and bite my tongue to stop me from saying that that's exactly what I'm doing.

Trey stays at the office for a little over thirty minutes as I get everything I need to set him up, ready to start on Monday. The moment the door closes behind him, I think I release the largest breath I've ever held.

How can this be fucking happening?

I know it's karma for everything that happened with Nick, I know it is, but it doesn't mean any of it is fair. I'm trying to prove to both Ben and Lauren that they were right in not firing me when the truth came out, but it's just got a load fucking harder if I'm going to have to spend my days being tortured by him.

CHAPTER FIVE

"YOU DUE ON your period or something? You've been a right moody bitch the past few days." I cut Joe a seething look, but it doesn't faze him at all.

"No. I'm not."

"So, what the fuck's wrong then. You haven't been yourself since last weekend. Oooh, is it the suit? Having withdrawal symptoms?"

"What? No. It was a one-night-stand. I got what I needed, and if he was lucky then so did he."

His eyes assess me, I guess to try to work out of I'm lying or not. "With the way you looked when you got in, I think it's safe to say he got what he needed."

I fight to keep the blush from my cheeks, it's not like me to get embarrassed so easily, but there was something about that guy. He's still under my skin, no matter how much I may protest to Joe that he's not. Joe is also totally oblivious that he's our new colleague. I made Lauren promise to keep it to herself, seeing as I have no intention of screwing anyone else who works for Johnson & Sons ever again.

"So what gives?"

"Nothing. I'm fine."

"Is your mum okay? Sam?" he asks, referring to my older sister.

"Yeah, everyone's good. Can you just leave it?"

He gives me a look that expresses how unhappy he is, but right now I don't really have the energy to give a fuck. My focus needs to be on work, one-hundred percent. I need to put all my energy into getting the new office set up and then into proving to both Ben and Lauren that I can fix the mess I helped make. I'm a huge part of the reason why we're moving offices and digging the company out of the hole. If I just had a little more integrity and was able to say no when Nick started helping me out, none of this would have happened.

"You need to get laid," Joe states, getting up and putting his empty plate into the dishwasher and heading towards his room. "And don't even think about asking me. I'm not sure I could live up to the suit." His shoulders shake with his laughter as he disappears. *Dickhead.*

Letting out a sigh, I drop my knife and fork and fall back into my chair. I hate feeling like this. I'm on edge all the time, worrying that something else I allowed to fall through the net at work is going to come back and bite me on the arse. It helps now that Joe's living here and helping me with the mortgage, but I can't lose my job and then ultimately my home. I've worked too hard, saved every penny I had spare to own my own place.

Scraping what's left on my plate into the bin, I throw it down on the counter and march towards my bedroom. Joe's right: getting laid would probably help lose some of my tension. It's just a shame that the only man I can picture fucking right now is one I really need to stay away from.

STARING INTO MY WARDROBE, I spend much longer than usual trying to decide what to wear to work. I usually put zero thought into it and drag out the first clean outfit I have, but it's a very different story this morning and I'm already irritated with myself that I care.

In the end, I settle on a pair of cut-off black trousers and a white shirt with a frill down the front. I ignore the little voice in my head that tells me my choice is solely based on the fact that the shirt gives me killer cleavage and instead focus on the fact that I think it makes me look slimmer.

My hair and make-up is done to perfection, and, as the seconds tick on the clock my nerves of what today is going to hold start to multiply.

It'll be fine. He'll just turn up, sit at his desk and get to work, I tell myself. He probably won't even look at me, let alone notice what I'm wearing.

"Whoa. You got a hot date after work or something?" Joe asks after doing a double take when he finds me in the kitchen a few minutes later.

"No, just trying to cheer myself up."

"So you admit something's wrong, then?" His eyebrow pops and I frown at him. "Fine, fine." With his hands up in defeat, he backs away, quickly snatching the travel mug I filled for him a few seconds ago. "I'll cook tonight, and I'll pick up your favourite pudding. Peace offering, yeah?"

"Whatever," I say nonchalantly, but the thought of digging into a New York cheesecake right now makes my mouth water. That should definitely help squash some of my cravings...*if I could eat it off his abs.*

Dragging my mind from the gutter, I grab a cereal bar from the cupboard and head out the way Joe went a few minutes ago. Unlike him, who's just jumped in a Johnson & Sons van to drive to site, I head down the road to the tube station to sit with hundreds of other Londoners on their commute into the city. My journey has more than doubled now I've got to get to Ben's house. It might be closer in distance, but on public transport it's a bitch and makes me mourn the loss of my car that little bit more.

By the time I push through the door of Ben's newly converted double garage, I'm a hot mess. Everyone's already here and all sets of eyes turn towards me as I stumble over the threshold.

"If that was meant to be a glamorous entrance, you failed," Ben says with a laugh, but he's the only one who's amused.

Lauren looks at me with concern laced through her features; no doubt Joe's told her what kind of mood I've been in all weekend. Then there's Trey. He stares at me like he's about to march over and fuck me against the wall. That image entering my head makes my temperature spike even more.

"Getting this side of town is a fucking nightmare," I mutter, eventually managing to break my stare with Trey and walk over to my new desk, which I now realise faces his. *Fuck my life.*

I keep my head down, not wanting to look into my colleagues' eyes. We all know it's partly my fault we're here right now. I don't need reminding of it once again.

"Get a coffee, Erica. We're meeting in ten."

"Sure thing, boss." I give him a quick salute and race towards the kitchenette. There isn't enough coffee in the world to help me get through today.

Ben, Lauren, Trey, and Jenny, Ben's mum, are already sitting around the giant table in the main office when I enter. "You're late. Take a seat," Ben barks, playing the part of being the boss perfectly. I manage to contain my proud smile and rush towards the closest empty seat. Unfortunately, the second I look up from said seat I realise my mistake. It's next to him.

I stop breathing the second his scent fills my nose and his eyes burn into my skin. I fight to ignore him and focus on opening my notebook, ready to take minutes.

Ben starts talking, but I've no fucking clue what about; I'm too lost to the feeling of Trey's body only inches away from mine.

My skin tingles and I watch out of the corner of my eyes as he leans towards me. Sucking in a lungful of air, I wait for what he's about to say.

"Nice shirt."

When I glance over, he's staring right at my tits, and I feel stupid for looking so obvious.

Shifting in my seat, I twist away from him and towards Ben, who's still chatting away, hopefully not about something I need to know.

The whole meeting, almost all my focus is on the man beside me. Thankfully, once I do manage to latch onto what Ben's talking about, I realise most of the information is about our current jobs and getting Trey up to date. I just hope he's able to pay more attention than I am.

"I think that's it. Trey, if you're okay, I'll take you out to a few of our sites now. Erica's got your phone and log on details on her desk. Grab all of that, then we'll head out, yeah?"

"You got it."

I'm out of that chair and then the office like the place is on fire. I continue past my desk and head for the toilet so I can have a minute or two to breathe.

I feel ridiculous for allowing him to affect me this much. He's just a guy. I've slept with plenty over the years; it's not like what I did last weekend was unusual.

What *is* unusual is how badly I want to be back in his bedroom again.

Resting my hands on the sink, I stare at myself in the mirror. I really need to get a grip.

He's sitting on the edge of my desk waiting for me when I eventually emerge. His dark grey trousers are stretched tight over his muscular thighs, giving me just a hint of what I know is hiding beneath. My mouth goes dry as desire ripples through me at the memory of just how tightly he filled me.

Lifting my eyes, I take in his black fitted shirt. It may as well be made to measure, the way it hugs his chest and strong arms. It's not until I get to his face that I realise I've been standing here checking him out for way too long. The smirk playing on his lips tells me that he knows exactly where my thoughts are.

His eyes dance over my body as I force thoughts of him naked from my head and make my way over to my desk.

Rolling my chair forward, I grab his phone and documents from my drawer. When I look again, he's leaning forward on my desk with his palms on the wood and his intense eyes on me.

Clearing my throat, I suck in a breath and attempt to do my job. "Here's your phone. I've already programmed in a lot of the numbers you'll need, and your email is already set up. Here are your computer log on details; the system will prompt you to change your password the first time you log on. You've also got a laptop on your desk." I nod my head towards where he's meant to sit, but he doesn't follow. Instead, his eyes stay locked on my tits. "Did you hear any of that?"

"Phone, password, laptop. Yeah, I think I got it. I think you've missed something, though."

"Oh?"

His eyes drop from mine once again. "I think I need a proper welcome to the office. You know, break in my desk and all that."

"I don't think that's necessary. The boss is waiting for you." Thankfully, at that moment Ben appears from his office and looks over at us. "Best you run along now."

"Fine. But I'll be back, and just so you know, that wasn't a suggestion. We *will* be christening my desk. Yours, too, if you're lucky."

My thighs clench at his words, but thankfully he turns and walks towards Ben and misses my reaction. He, on the other hand, looks totally unaffected about the prospect of fucking me a mere few feet from where the boss lives.

"What are the plans for tonight, then?" Lauren asks after we've finished eating our lunch.

"Uh..."

"You *have* planned a night out, right? It's what you do when a new member of staff starts."

I had a feeling this was going to bite me in the arse. Lauren knows me too well, but luckily for me, I have the perfect excuse to ensure I don't have to end up on another night out with Trey.

"Nope. There are age restrictions, remember?"

"Seriously? You're not organising drinks tonight because Trey is over your thirty-five age limit." Her eyebrows rise, and I think she's expecting me to tell her she's joking any minute.

"Seriously. He's too old."

"Didn't stop you fucking him though, did it?" Her voice is full of amusement as she reminds me once again of my mistake.

"Touché."

"I guess I'll have to take matters into my own hands."

"W-what does that mean?"

"He's here to help save this place." I wince, knowing what she means although her voice holds no accusation. "So the least we owe him is a night out." Rolling my eyes, I go to argue. "Don't even think about finding an excuse to get out of it."

CHAPTER SIX

THE MORE THE week goes on, the worse my mood gets. It's all my own fault and my inability to get my head out of the gutter whenever I'm forced to look at Trey.

Thankfully, Ben's kept him pretty busy with site visits, but he's been in the office almost all day today and I'm practically vibrating with the need for release. He hasn't even really done anything to wind me up, just walking past my desk and filling the air around me with his scent is enough. I feel like a horny fucking teenager and I don't like it. I should be able to control my desire, but, at this point, I fear the only thing that's going to dampen it is him.

It's Thursday afternoon and Trey's in Ben's office. They've got the door shut, but the rumble of his deep, gravelly voice still filters through to me, leaving me sitting here squirming.

The main door opens, catching my attention, and when I turn to look I find a very dirty Joe walking in.

"Had a good day?" I ask with a laugh.

"Yeah, great. Will pulled a ceiling down on my head."

"Shouldn't you be at home showering? Ahh, get the fuck away from me," I squeal when he comes over like he's about to hug me."

"Glad to see you're in a better mood," he says with a laugh as he rounds my desk and drops into the seat at the other side. "Apparently we're all going out Friday night. If you're lucky, your suit might be at the bar. Hopefully another round or two with him will—"

I stop listening when I spot the office door opening behind Joe's shoulder. I pray that it's going to be Ben who steps out, but because this is me and my luck is so shitty, of course it's Trey who emerges, a shit-eating grin on his face.

His eyes land on mine, amusement making them look more silver than their usual dark steel.

Joe's still talking, but my panic as well as the effect Trey's stare has on my body means I don't hear a word of it. When Trey's smile only gets wider, I know it can't be anything good.

"Is that right?" Trey's gruff voice fills the room, and it brings me back from my daze.

I break my stare on him just in time to see Joe turn to see who's behind him.

His chin drops before he exclaims, "Holy shit." He turns back to me before looking back to Trey again. "Now it's all starting to make sense," he chuckles. "So you didn't fancy telling me that the 'best shag of your life' now works in this exact office?"

"I...uh...fuck." Joe narrows his eyes. Disappointment oozes from him that I've kept this to myself. All the while, Trey's eyes continue to lighten with amusement.

"Joe, can you...What's going on?" Ben asks when he sticks his head out of his office and looks between the three of us.

"Probably best you don't know. You ready?"

"Yeah." He doesn't sound very positive as he pulls the office door closed, still looking between us like we're a puzzle he needs to work out.

After a couple of seconds, both Ben and Joe leave the office. Glancing around, I realise for the first time that everyone else has left for the day. My heart thunders and my palms start to sweat. Being alone in a room with this man is not a good idea, especially with the way he's staring down at me right now.

"I-I need...I need to leave."

"Why? You got somewhere better to be?"

"Uh..." I rack my brain for a smart answer, the kind that would usually fall from my mouth right about now, but while I'm captive in his grey eyes, my brain refuses to work. "Home," I squeak when his lips curl into a smirk and I'm forced to say something.

"How about I join you."

"What? No, that wasn't an invitation."

"No? Your little friend seems to think it'll be a good idea." He rounds the desk and I roll my chair back in my pathetic attempt to keep some distance between us.

"He...he doesn't know what he's talking about."

"Really? He sounded like he knew *exactly* what would fix your current mood. And I must say, I agree with him."

My chair hits the wall and I scramble out of it. My body screams "Yes!" as I do anything I can to stay far enough away from him, but thankfully my head's winning the fight right now. I can't let him touch me again. Just the memory of it has been haunting me. I can only imagine how bad it'll become if I allow myself to experience him again.

"Trey, we can't do this." My sensible side shows herself, and I continue backing away. We're at work, the place where I should be proving myself, not allowing the new guy to put his hands on me. We can't do this.

I can't do this.

"It's only you fighting it, sweetheart."

The disappointment that haunts Lauren's eyes every time she looks at me pops into my head. I can't let her down again. *I can't.*

"Trey, please." His eyes flash with desire. "No, I wasn't. Please." *Fuck,* even to my own ears it sounds like I'm begging him.

My back hits the wall, and I panic when I drag my eyes from his and realise that he's backed me into a corner.

My chest heaves, desire sitting heavy in my lower stomach, and my clit starts to pound from the memories of his touch alone.

"It's funny, because every time you say that it sounds like you want it more."

"Trey." It's no more than a moan as he takes one last step towards me. His scent fills my nose and my mouth waters for a taste of him, to feel his tongue dancing with mine, to feel the heat of his hands on my skin.

"You need to stop denying yourself what you want, because we both know exactly what that is."

His heat burns my front as he closes the space between us. Ripping my eyes away from him, I stare down at the floor, hoping it'll be enough to convince us both that this isn't about to happen. He's silent for a beat before a low and deep chuckle rumbles up his throat. His fingers find my chin and my head is moved so I have no choice but to look at him.

"You've been thinking about kissing me again since the moment you walked out, haven't you?"

"No." My voice doesn't sound as strong as I was hoping. His eyebrow lifts in amusement.

"So your temperature doesn't spike every time you look at me? Your clit doesn't throb for my touch every time I'm close?"

"Nope, neither."

His eyes shine with delight as they flit between mine and my lips.

"Just as I thought."

I don't get a chance to say any more before his lips are on mine and his tongue is in my mouth. My breath catches and I sag back against the wall. *Jesus,* no man has ever managed to consume me quite like him before.

His hips pin me to the wall, his solid length pressing into my stomach, and my need for more starts to get the better of me. Lifting my hand, I grip onto his muscular upper arms as his hands skim down my body.

A little squeal passes my lips when he bites down

on my bottom one before moving across my jaw and down my neck, allowing me a few minutes to drag in some much needed air.

He sucks on the sensitive skin beneath my ear as his fingers find the bottom of my skirt.

My surroundings vanish as his fingertips tickle their way up my bare thighs. The only thing I can focus on is where they're heading.

"Fuck," he grunts when he slips my soaked knickers aside and runs his fingers through my folds.

"Holy shit," falls from my lips as he slides two inside me.

"Are you ready to admit you were lying yet?"

"Fuck, Trey." My chest heaves as my release starts to grow closer.

"I won't let you come until you tell me that you want me, that you fall asleep at night wishing I'd been inside you."

"No, no," I chant, although I've no idea what I'm really saying. All I know is that his fingers and deep voice are exactly what I need right now.

"Erica," he warns seconds before pulling his fingers from me.

"I-I...*fuck*." The office door flies open and Lauren walks in, totally unaware of what's going on only feet away from her.

"Shit. I...oh..." She quickly looks to the other side

of the room, and Trey takes a step back. Coldness engulfs me, but it soon vanishes when I look back to Lauren.

I've let her down again. My stomach twists in frustration with myself for not being able to do the right thing.

"I'm so sorry," I whisper before rushing towards my desk, grabbing my bag and running from the office. I can't hang around and see that look in her eye. I already hate myself for everything I've done to her; I don't need to make it any worse.

Finding a taxi idling down the street, I jump in and give the driver my address, forgetting about the cost. Money isn't my biggest concern right now.

My body's still wound tight as I make my way up the stairs to my flat. Pushing the door open, I head straight for my room and slam it behind me. My chest heaves from running up the stairs, but it's still mostly from the desire still coursing through my body as I remember the feeling of Trey's fingers stretching me open.

"Fuck." Dropping my head into my hands, I scream out my frustration. Why can't I just find a decent bloke to settle down with? I've always known my addiction to bad boys with bad attitudes was going to get me hurt, but I never could have predicted the mess my life has become.

I thought I'd found the one with my ex. He seemed like the perfect mix of bad boy on the outside and kind on the in. Until it turned out it was all an act, and he was just an arsehole through and through who was up to his eyeballs in debt. I was distraught the day he left, but bad soon turned to worse when the final demands and bailiffs started turning up at my door. It turned out it wasn't only him who was drowning, because he'd put my name and address on a load of his debts. I'd worked my arse off saving for this place over the years, and because of him I was on the verge of losing it. That was when the other arsehole stepped in to help ruin my life just a little bit more.

Not wanting to think about Nick and how he manipulated me so easily into doing whatever he wanted, I push myself from the door and walk towards my en suite. I need to wash today off me.

Sadly, no length of shower is going to allow me to forget him. He's well and truly under my skin, and the fucker knows it.

I stand under the spray of the water long after I've used all the hot.

Pulling on a pair of old leggings and an oversized jumper, I head out into the kitchen to make myself some comfort food.

I'm just digging into my macaroni cheese when

the front door opens and Joe appears. His face is still minging when he looks up at me, although slightly less so than earlier.

"I can't believe you didn't tell me the suit is our new contracts manager. When were you planning on fessing up, exactly?" His disappointment is obvious in his voice, and it only makes me feel worse than I already do. I'm fed up of disappointing people, but it seems to be all I'm capable of these days.

"I don't know," I whisper. "I didn't exactly expect this to happen. I had no idea until he turned up the following Monday with his ID and shit."

"You've known that long and didn't tell me?"

"I didn't know what to say. My main focus has been not fucking up again, but how long did that last? A few weeks at best?"

"You weren't to know."

"But I know now."

"So? It's not like he's Lauren's dad." My chin drops and my eyes harden. "Too soon for jokes?"

"It'll forever be too soon to joke about that."

"Seriously, Erica. This isn't a big deal. So what, you spend your nights fantasising about the new guy. There's no reason why you can't."

"I just want to show Ben and Lauren that I'm serious, and this isn't the way to go about it."

Reaching over he takes my hand in his dirty one.

"They know, Erica. If they had any concerns, they would have let you go, but they haven't. You still have a job, and they're still your friends. Trust them. Trust *yourself*."

Blowing out a breath, I try to force the words he's just said to settle inside me. I'm still on edge after the encounter earlier, and anything short of having his hands on me to finish the job—which isn't happening —isn't going to relax me.

"I need to go and shower, but do you want to go for drinks after?"

I stare at him, weighing up my options. Sit in here and replay everything with Trey over and over, or go and attempt to forget about it.

"We're going. Get your arse up and put something sexy on." Joe's authoritative tone leaves no room for argument, and I follow his instruction.

CHAPTER SEVEN

GOING out with Joe didn't really help. He tried his best to keep me entertained and to stop my mind from wandering, but no matter how hard I tried, Trey was still there in my head and under my skin. It's going to take a lot more than a couple of glasses of alcohol to get rid of him, that's for sure.

Much to my relief, Trey's hardly in the office on Friday. He's either out on site or locked in the office with Ben going over stuff that doesn't involve me, thank fuck. The least amount of time I can spend in an enclosed space with him the better.

"I've got a table booked at Blueprint for seven-thirty. Do not be late," Lauren warns, perching herself on the edge of my desk sometime late that afternoon once everyone else has left.

"I...uh..."

"Don't even think about it, Erica. We're all going out together. It'll be good for everyone."

Rolling my eyes, I rest back in my chair and cross my arms over my chest. "Are we just going to pretend last night didn't happen?"

"If you want to. You didn't look like you wanted to talk about it."

Dropping my head back on a sigh, I try to find the words. "I really don't want to talk about it, but I'm...I'm sorry. I just keep fucking up, and I don't—"

"It's okay." Dragging my head forward, I find her soft blue eyes and my own fill with tears that I refuse to cry.

"It's not, though. I need to be working, righting my wrongs, trying to make shit up to you...and here I am getting caught with the new guy's fingers inside me."

"Okay, so that wasn't ideal, but you're not fucking up, E. Trey's hot; anyone with eyes can see that, and he seems to have a bit of a fascination with you. I would never blame you for testing that out. Who knows where it could lead."

"Probably with me fucking another member of staff and getting what I deserve."

"And what is it you think you deserve?"

"For you to hate me." Reaching out, she grasps my shoulders in a show of support.

"Out of everyone, I'm the one who understands what you went through the most. Of course I don't like it, but I also get that what happened with my dad was not your fault. He was a master manipulator, and I should be apologising to you for not seeing what was going on. He was cooking my books right under my nose and disrespecting my best friend at the same time. I hate myself for not seeing any of that. I knew *exactly* how much you were struggling after Matt left, and I should have been a better friend. I should have been the one to help dig you out, not him. I just—"

I don't allow her to say any more. Standing, I throw my arms around her shoulders and hold her tight. We've spoken about this before, but today I think I'm finally starting to accept that what she's saying is true. I'll forever blame myself for allowing that situation to happen in the first place, and for hurting Lauren when she was already going through so much shit, but I think I'm getting somewhere.

"Thank you," I say when I pull back from her.

She grabs my hands to stop me walking away—not that I was going to. "You are coming tonight, aren't you? Please don't think that I'll stop you doing anything with Trey. You never know, he might be *the one*." I can't help but laugh at her. "What? He's totally your type. Brooding, hot, a bit of an arsehole on the surface but a total teddy bear beneath.”

“How do you know what’s beneath?” My brows draw together, making Lauren laugh.

“I can just tell. He’s a good guy, Erica. Give it a chance.”

“And what if it doesn’t work? What if I fuck it up again and one of us has to leave?”

“Stop worrying about the what ifs. For once, just enjoy it without worrying about the consequences.”

That’s easier said than done. I’ve experienced the fallout more than once for acting without considering what might happen when it all goes wrong. I’ve also been fooled by the ones I thought were hard on the outside and soft in the middle. Those arseholes are good at getting what they want and then showing their full colours when it’s too late.

“Stop worrying.”

The main office door opens and Ben and Trey walk in, both immediately looking our way where we’re still standing with our hands together.

“Looks like we turned up at just the right time,” Ben says with a wink. “Please continue.” His eyes flick between us as he leans back against the wall as if he’s waiting for a show.

“You’re a pig,” Lauren says, trying to sound as

serious as possible, but amusement fills her voice as she steps away from me.

I don't see her go. I only know she's reached Ben when he complains about her hitting him; I'm too lost in the steel eyes that haven't left me since they entered.

"Seven-thirty, Erica." She goes to leave but stops in the doorway. "And you should totally wear that little red dress you've got. It'll work like a charm." She's gone before I can respond. Trey has no idea what my red dress might look like, but already his eyes are darkening and the muscles in his neck are tensing.

Nope, I will not allow him to consume me, I tell myself as I turn back to my computer. *Tonight, I will stay out of his way. And I will go home alone.*

BY THE TIME I'm standing at the entrance to Blueprint in my little red dress, my stomach is full of butterflies and my hands are trembling.

"Will you chill out? I can't cope with you like this, it's weird," Joe complains, threading his arm through mine and all but dragging me inside. "Have I mentioned how hot you look? I'm kinda jealous it's all for him."

"Shut up, you idiot." Shaking my head at him, a little laugh falls from my lips.

"What? It's been a while since I've had any action."

"Enough."

Joe and I have had a fumble about a time or two when we were in need of a little tension release, and while I like to not dwell on getting freaky with one of my best friends and flatmate, he likes to bring it up as often as possible just to make me squirm. I was confused as fuck the first time he leaned in a kissed me after a night out, because I was convinced he was gay. I'd only ever seen him with men up until that point, but shit, he kissed me like he knew exactly what to do with a woman. He also wasn't shy when we got down to it and he got me off in record time. I always thought a body like that was a waste, but knowing a woman could put it to good use did make me feel a little better. If he wasn't one of my closest friends, I might have wanted more, but as much as I love him, romance is most definitely not in our future. I've heard and witnessed him with too many others to even consider it.

I'm practically vibrating with nervous energy by the time we're pointed towards the table. I tell myself that he won't be here yet and that I'll have a few minutes to get settled, but the second we round the corner, I see that none of that will be happening because we're last.

The second Lauren spots us approaching, she calls Joe over and he happily takes the seat next to her leaving only one free.

Rolling my eyes at her antics, I take a step towards the vacant chair but my shoe catches on a bump on the floor and I stumble. Thankfully, Trey sees what's about to happen, and moments before I'm expecting to get extra friendly with the floor tiles, his giant hands land on my waist. Electric sparks shoot around my body and my skin burns where we're touching.

Keeping my eyes on the floor, I mumble a thank you, aware that everyone's silent around us.

"Erica?" he breathes moments before his finger presses under my chin and forces my head up so I have no choice but to look at him. His dark eyes are full of concern, but his lips are pulled up in a sexy smirk.

He feels the connection between us, too.

He leans in and I suck in a breath, thinking he's going to kiss me right here in front of everyone, but at the last minute he moves to the side so he can whisper in my ear.

"I'm taking that dress off you tonight...with my teeth."

My thighs clench and my clit throbs at the thought. A flush the colour of my dress heats my cheeks and neck. He pulls back and returns to his chair as if nothing's happened. I glance over at Lauren as I go to take my seat, and her eyes are full of delight and mischief. I narrow mine at her, hoping she realises how much I don't appreciate her meddling, but all she does is laugh.

I sit ramrod straight in my chair, afraid of what I'll do if I allow myself to relax. My entire body is being called to the one next to me.

Everyone goes back to their previous conversations while I stare at the menu, but it's as if it's written in another language because the only things I can focus on are his hands on my body and his hot breath against my ear.

"You can't stop thinking about it, can you?"

"Don't know what you're talking about." I refuse to look at him or let him see that I'm affected by his words in any way, although I fear it may be a little too late for that.

"What do you fancy?" He nods his head towards the menu. I almost think he's asking a serious question until his fingers brush against my bare thigh beneath the table.

Knocking it away, I turn to him. "I don't know. Are you allergic to anything?"

The silver in his eyes immediately becomes obvious and his lips curl into the most incredible smile as he barks out a laugh. "Sorry to disappoint you, but even that wouldn't stop me."

"Shame. What are you having?" I don't particularly care what his dish of choice might be, but I need to get onto safer ground, especially when I can feel multiple sets of eyes burning into me.

"What I'm eating tonight's not on this menu."

Heat fills my belly and descends to my core. *Fucking hell.*

"I-I was thinking lasagne," I stutter, hoping no one else around the table heard him. His laughter once again hits my ears and my stomach does a little flip. My head might be telling me to stay as far away from this man as possible, but it's very obvious that the rest of my body is totally on board with everything he has to offer.

The sexual tension is so thick between us that I can barely breathe. Everyone around us is either oblivious or they're ignoring it. They chat away about work and life like normal while I sit here, trying not to melt into a puddle on the seat at just being able to feel his body heat.

Every few seconds his eyes flick over to me, but I refuse to return his stare, too afraid of what I might do or suggest if I look into them.

He lowers his cutlery to his plate and drops his hands from the table once he's finished eating. I think nothing of it until the continued movement of his arm catches my eye seconds before his fingertips trail up my thigh once again.

I suck in a breath, successfully managing to inhale a bit of my lasagne at the same time. Coughing, I manage to drag the attention of everyone at our table, but at no point does Trey remove his hand from me—in fact, he uses my coughing fit to turn into me so not only can he start touching me up, but he can tap me on the back to look like he's assisting.

"I'm good, thanks," I mutter when he continues hitting my back long after I've finished.

"You sure will be." The promise in his voice makes my thighs clench. His lips curl the moment he feels it, and it gives him the encouragement he needs.

Thinking the show's over, everyone turns away from us, giving Trey the opportunity he needs to slide his hand higher.

I once again suck in a breath when his fingers brush against the lace of my underwear.

"Trey," I warn quietly. "Don't."

"Don't pretend you don't need this. You're fucking soaked." I can't deny what he's saying is true, but we can't do this in the middle of a busy restaurant with our friends and colleagues sitting only feet away.

"I...shit," I gasp as he slips his finger beneath the lace. "Trey," I whimper.

When I look up, I find Lauren staring right at me, a small smile on her lips telling me she knows exactly what's going on, but all she does is wink at me and turn away to give us some privacy, if that's even possible right now.

Trey presses harder against my clit and I almost jump out of my chair.

"Did you get yourself off when you got home last night?" His low, rumbling voice does little to stop the pressure building between my legs.

"I might have."

He groans in response and my chest puffs out a little, knowing how torturous this is for him. I know that if I were to reach out, I'd find him hard as steel beneath his trousers.

I bite down on my bottom lip as I recall exactly what that looks like.

"You're imagining me naked, aren't you?" My head snaps to him. How does he know that? "I can read every thought in your dirty mind right now, Miss Wilde."

My mouth opens to respond, but his fingers circle my clit, edging me closer towards my release.

Pushing lower, he circles my entrance with one finger before sliding it inside me as far as it'll go with me sitting in this position. He ups the ante and pushes a second inside, and the sensation of being filled by him once again causes my orgasm to crash into me. I grip onto the edge of the table, my fingernails digging into the wood as I fight to keep my lips shut and not draw more attention to myself than I'm sure I already have.

The second my release subsides and I can instruct my legs to move, I get up and practically run for the toilets. I don't dare look up for fear of what I'm going to see on everyone's faces.

The door flies open as I slam into it, making it crash back against the wall. I race into one of the cubicles and lock myself inside.

Putting the toilet lid down, I fall onto it and drop my head into my hands.

What the fuck am I doing?

My heart pounds and my chest heaves as I try to get my breathing back under control. I can't believe I just allowed him to do that. I'm such a fucking idiot. I told myself I'd stay away from him yet less than an hour at that table and he's already completely consumed me. I swear there's something seriously fucking wrong with me.

I've no idea how long I sit there chastising myself

for my stupid behaviour, but eventually the door squeaks open and footsteps sound out. I expect to hear Lauren's voice, but no one says anything.

Silence fills the air until water runs at the sinks. Footsteps sound out again before the door squeaks and, thinking I'm safe, I unlock my own door and walk out. I only make it two steps before the body leaning back against the sinks like he owns the fucking place makes my legs stop working.

"Thought I was going to have to come in and get you."

"W-what are you doing?"

"Having my dessert."

I don't get the chance to respond, because he's on me. His fingers slide into my hair and move my head to the perfect angle so his lips can crash down on mine and his tongue can plunge into my mouth.

A moan rumbles up my throat at feeling his hard body pressed up against mine. I'm powerless to do anything but submit to his demands and slide my hands around to cup his arse. The move brings us closer still, and his solid length presses into my stomach.

"This fucking dress," he moans, running his finger down the front until he's at my cleavage. Slipping the fabric aside, he pushes my bra down and sucks my puckered nipple into his mouth. A loud moan crawls up my throat and I shamelessly thrust my breasts towards him, needing more of his touch.

"Put your hands on the counter and stick your arse out." Stumbling away from him on shaky legs, I do as instructed with no concern about where we are or who could walk in. The only thing on my mind is him and what he's about to do.

The release he gave me at the table was just a tease of what's to come. I knew that at the time. Men like Trey don't settle for just that; they want it all.

The fabric of my skirt is flipped over my back, exposing my bare arse.

"Fuck," Trey grunts, running his finger along with scrap of lace between my arse cheeks. "Even better than I remember."

"Trey, please," I beg. My pussy clenches around nothing as he rubs me over the fabric of my knickers. "Please." I'm so fucking wet and ready for him that I should be embarrassed, but right now, as long as he slides his length into me, I don't give a fuck. I need this. I've needed this since the moment I walked out of his flat last weekend.

It seems like forever, but eventually the sound of his belt and trousers being undone fills the room. Heat floods my core and I wait impatiently.

His growl of pleasure bounces off the walls around us as he slides into me. My muscles greedily pull him deeper, needing to remember what it felt like when I was full to the hilt with him.

"Yes," he hisses when he's as deep as he can go and nudging at my womb.

He slowly pulls out and it just about gives me the time I need to lock my arms and prepare for the thrust I know is coming. I'm right; he slams back into me, forcing me forward and into the marble surrounding the sink. His fingers dig into my hips as he helps hold me up, obviously aware that he was going to turn me into a rag doll in seconds.

He thrusts into me with punishing blows that hit the exact spot I need over and over. It's only minutes before the tingles of my release start to hit.

"Fuck. Fuck your pussy, fuck," he roars, his length swelling inside me before his hot cum fills me.

"Uh..."

"I really fucking needed that."

Folding his large body over me, he places his lips to my neck and kisses as his breathing begins to slow.

What the actual fuck? My pussy is still convulsing and my clit pounding, waiting to find the release I crave.

His arms wrap around my waist, and I stand so my back is to his front. His cock slips out of me and I immediately feel lost, like I missing a part of who I am.

"Fuck, I don't want to let you go." The honesty in his words has me pulling away from him, even though in reality it's the last thing I want to do. I might be frustrated to hell right now, but still, it would be so easy to fall for him, to grow attached, but that only leads to pain. I need to keep a clear head about this and remember what it is—a quick fling. He'll soon be bored of me and move onto someone more interesting, more successful and with fewer skeletons hiding in her closet.

"That's it?" I ask when he starts doing up his trousers.

"Yep. You got yours at the table. This was for me."

"But—"

"If you're lucky, maybe I'll let you have another."

I splutter in astonishment, but I can't deny that I'm already planning just how to make that happen.

Turning my back to him, right my clothing and then wash my hands in cold water, hoping that it'll help to cool my heated body. It doesn't work; with his eyes burning into my back, there's nothing that could cool me down.

"Erica?" Placing his hand on my forearm, I'm forced to look up at him. Concern flashes in his eyes but it's gone in an instant, the solid and demanding demeanour I'm becoming used to slipping back into place.

"I need to get back."

"That's it? Not even a thank you?" There's amusement in his tone, but I know it's forced.

"Thanks for nothing. It shouldn't have happened, but...it did."

When I get to the door and pull the handle I realise why we weren't interrupted; he must have flicked the lock when he entered.

CHAPTER EIGHT

THE SECOND I appear around the corner, Lauren clocks me and elbows Ben in the ribs, who immediately gets up and starts walking my way.

"You okay?" he whispers.

"Of course." His eyes narrow before they quickly scan my face. He doesn't believe a word of it, and I'm sure my appearance right now doesn't really help.

He nods before walking past me and towards the toilets right as Trey exits. I should be embarrassed, but something tells me that Ben already knew exactly what was going on just a few feet down the hall. I continue watching as he stops right in front of Trey, his arm against the wall as if he's caging him in to ensure he listens to every word he's about to say.

Rushing towards Lauren, I sit myself in Ben's vacant seat. "What the hell is he doing?"

"What he's good at."

"And what's that exactly?"

"Well, there are a few things," she admits with a salacious look in her eyes, "but right now he's just being protective."

"He doesn't need to protect me."

"Maybe not, but he wants to. Just let him do his thing."

"Fine," I mumble, although I'm anything but happy about him getting involved.

"Sooo...have fun in the toilets?"

"I don't know what you're talking about."

"Oh, come off it, E. You were totally just fucking him in there." Everyone around the table is suddenly silent, and my cheeks heat as every set of eyes finds me. Most are amused by Lauren's announcement that came at just the perfect moment as the music dropped out, but none more so than Joe's.

"Oh, just fuck off. Don't even pretend you're not all jealous."

"I'm so sorry," Lauren whispers when everyone starts to return to their previous conversations, although some of them seem to be keeping an eye on me.

"It's fine. They all think I'm a slut for sleeping with the boss, so I may as well play up to it."

"They do not think that."

I'm about to argue, but two shadows fall over the table. Looking up, I find Ben with his shoulders pulled tight with tension. He really is in full-on protective mode.

"I'm a big girl, I can look after myself," I whisper in his ear once I'm on my feet.

"I know, but you shouldn't have to."

I give him a quick hug, because although I'm a little pissed that he felt the need to do whatever it was he just did, I do kinda like that he cares enough to look out for me.

He returns my hug, but my grip on him falters when I find Trey's eyes over his shoulder. Ben might be my boss and one of my best and oldest friends, but his normally steel orbs are almost green with jealousy.

Releasing Ben, I head back over to my empty chair and he follows, although no words are exchanged between us.

The tension's thick as we eat our desserts and pay the bill. Everyone keeps a close eye on both of us; I'm not sure what they're expecting, for us to hop up on the table and fuck in the middle of a busy restaurant, or something?

"The Avenue?" Joe asks the group. Most agree, but a couple of the guys who have families decline in favour of heading home.

Standing to leave, Trey's hand lands in the small of my back. His heat radiates through me, and I hate how much I love the feeling. My heart rate increases once again, knowing what those fingers are capable of.

We're only just outside the restaurant when his phone starts ringing. Pulling it out of his pocket, he looks down at the screen and winces. "I'm sorry, I need to take this."

"WHERE DID LOVER BOY GO?" Joe asks me when I slide in next to him at the bar.

"He got a phone call and had to leave." My frustration of knowing I'm not getting what I need anytime soon gets the better of me.

"Well, I guess he's already got lucky, no need to hang around until the end of the night," he quips.

"You're a twat."

"You've got it bad for him, haven't you?"

"I don't know what you're talking about. I haven't got anything for him."

He opens his mouth to say more, but the look I pin him with has his hands rising in surrender. Instead of berating me about my little bathroom session at the restaurant, he slides a shot towards me, encouraging me to down it before taking my hand and leading me to the dancefloor. "Dance so we get some attention. I really need to get lucky tonight."

Yeah, you and me both.

I slide my hands up his chest and lock them around the back of his neck. Our hips move in time to the music, and it's only a few minutes later when I notice both male and female eyes checking out Joe's arse. He should be in for a good night.

"Toilet break?" Lauren shouts in my ear once Joe's turned and started grinding with someone else, leaving me like a gooseberry with her and Ben.

"Yes."

She gives Ben a kiss on the cheek before taking my hand and dragging me towards the ladies'. We each manage to find an empty cubicle to do our thing before meeting back up at the sinks.

"You okay?" she asks me in the mirror.

"Yeah, why?"

"What happened to Trey?"

"No idea. He had to go deal with something. No biggie."

"Really?" Her eyebrow quirks up and she turns to me.

"Really. It's not like we're a couple or anything."

"Hmm..."

"What?"

"I'm pretty sure he wants you to be."

"No, I'm pretty sure he just wants the excitement of fucking me in the restaurant toilets."

"I can't believe you did that," she giggles, showing that she's had a little too much to drink.

"Like you can say anything. You can't tell me you and Ben haven't done it anywhere you shouldn't." Her face flames bright red. If it weren't for the two of them being my best friends and having to see them every day, I might ask for details, but in reality I really don't need any kind of visual in my head, especially if it involved the office.

Thankfully, my phone buzzes in my bag and I pull it out, hoping to put an end to the conversation.

My brows pinch when I find a message from an unknown number. Curiosity gets the better of me and I swipe the screen to see what it is. Expecting it to be spam, my chin drops when I find an address staring back at me. It's one I know very well, and although my body aches for more of him, I know I won't be following his demands.

"Booty call?" Lauren asks innocently.

"Yeah, actually."

Turning my phone, I allow her to read the address. "Wait. That address is—"

"I know. It's fucking torture." A wide smile splits her face before she starts laughing and drags me from the toilets, exclaiming that we need another drink. It's something I can't argue with.

While she shouts our order at the barman, I pull my phone back out and send a response.

> Erica: If you think I take well to orders, you really don't know me at all.

Feeling smug, I slide my phone back into my bag and take the drink Lauren hands me.

"What?" she asks, noticing my expression.

"Nothing, nothing. I just replied to my booty call."

"I don't want to know."

My phone vibrates again. I want to ignore it so he doesn't think I'm waiting for a reply when it comes up that it's been read so quickly, but I'm too damn nosey not to see what he's said.

Swiping the screen, I stare down at his words.

> Trey: You followed orders perfectly well when you were in my bed.

"Fuck," I mutter to myself as heat rushes to my core. Of course, he's right. I fucking *loved* following his orders.

The promise of what I could find at the address sitting on my phone has me ready and raring to go for the rest of our time in the club, but as much as I might want another roll around in his bed, the sensible thing to do is to stay as far away as possible. I've already screwed up twice tonight, I've already had my fill of mistakes, and I know going to him would surely be one.

"Why are you staring at the stairs so longingly?" Joe asks once we've stumbled our way to our floor.

"N-no reason."

"What happened to the woman you were dancing with?"

"She went home with her boyfriend."

"Oh. Ouch."

"I think I'm destined to be celibate forever. Call it karma or some shit for all the lies I've told."

"You think your lack of action is punishment for lying to Lauren?"

"It must be. I'm a total catch and never had any problems before."

"Maybe it's the arrogance that turns people off," I suggest as he steps aside to allow me into the flat. I immediately reach down and pull my heels from my feet, dropping them to the floor, sighing with relief.

"Nah, doubt that. So how about it? You're horny and drunk, and I'm desperate. Little bit of tickling, little bit of sucking, and we can both go to sleep satisfied?"

I stare at him, trying to figure out if he's serious or not, but when all I get is a hopeful expression staring back at me, I bark out a laugh.

"Wow, you sure know how to make a girl feel special, Joe."

"Oh, I can make you feel special all right. You remember how I did that thing—"

"Yeah, I remember, but I'm sorry. I'm not the girl for you tonight." As much as I might need more than I've already had, hooking up with Joe is the last thing I should be doing right now. This is one decision I know I'm not going to screw up. "It's just you and your right hand, big man."

"Cock tease," he jokes as he heads towards his room.

I do the same, and in only minutes I'm sliding between my cold covers. The alcohol flowing through my system mixes with the desire that's been simmering for the past few hours, and before I know what I'm doing my fingers find their way into my knickers to try to relieve the pressure that's built up to an intolerable level.

Not getting the results as quickly as I'd like, I reach over for my top drawer to pull out my little friend, but as I pull the drawer open my phone catches my eye. Feeling brazen, I grab it and hit call on the number that messaged me earlier. I put it on speaker as it rings, place it on my pillow and grab my vibrator. The phone rings loud into the room and my stomach drops with disappointment when it goes to voicemail...until an idea forms in my head.

Flicking the switch on my vibrator, I throw the covers back, shimmy my knickers down and press it to my clit. The new batteries I put in it the other day means it's extra powerful, and my breath catches in surprise. I soon get used to it and my hips start to roll with my need for more. A moan falls from my lips as my long awaited release starts making itself known. Making sure I'm putting on a show, I drop my other hand between my legs and plunge two fingers into my heat.

"Ah fuck," I moan before continuing to fuck myself. "Can you hear that? I'm gonna make myself come so hard. I don't need to cave to your demands to get what I need. I don't need your cock when I can do this myself." My breathy voice continues to explain what I'm doing and nail the point home that I don't need him—or any man, for that matter.

I call out his name as my orgasm rolls through me. It's nowhere near as strong as the one he gave me earlier, but like fuck am I telling him that. My entire body is limp with exhaustion by the time I pull my vibrator away and drop it on my bedside table. I end the call on my phone, roll over, and almost instantly fall into a deep sleep.

CHAPTER NINE

MY MUSCLES PULL and my head pounds when I roll over the next morning. Little flashes of the night before play out in my mind and I groan, knowing that I embarrassed myself once again.

Dragging my body up to sit against the headboard, I look over to my bedside table, hoping that I was sensible enough to at least get a glass of water before passing out, but no such luck.

Something cold hits my leg, and when I reach down my fingers wrap around my phone. The screen lights up and I find a missed call and four messages.

"Oh fuck." Rushing to unlock it, I drop the phone to the duvet and curse myself for drinking so much last night.

Ignoring the missed call, I go straight for the

messages. My breath catches the moment I see the dick pic staring back at me. My hand flies to my mouth in shock and my eyes widen in delight. Even with his hand wrapped around it, it's fucking impressive. My core clenches and regret fills me that I didn't follow orders last night. I could have been waking up in his arms right now, not just staring at a picture of his cock.

Underneath the picture are two messages. The first is his address again, the second is one single word...*Waiting*.

Fuck if he doesn't know exactly how to get me going. I'm tempted to have another session with my battery operated friend, but when I see another message sitting on my phone from Lauren asking me to brunch, I push the idea aside and drag my sore body from the bed in favour of getting freshened up to go and gossip with my friend. I need someone to put my head on straight. Getting into something with Trey is a bad idea, and I need someone beside me to nail the point home.

Stripping out of my vest and knickers, I wait for the shower to heat and then step underneath, hoping the hot spray will help wash some of my tension away. That picture sitting on my phone is still front and centre of my mind. I need to do something to get rid of it—something besides following orders and sitting on it.

After getting myself a mug of coffee, I spend a ridiculous amount of time drying and curling my hair in an attempt to pass some time before I need to meet Lauren. I apply my make-up flawlessly, telling myself that it's pointless because under no circumstances am I going to end up at his flat.

After pulling on a black V-neck jumper and my favourite red and black tartan skirt, I dump my mug in the sink and tug my knee-length boots on my feet.

Just as I'm about to pull the front door open, Joe appears looking worse for wear from his bedroom.

"You look too good for this time of the morning," he mutters, running his hand through his messed up hair.

"It's gone ten."

"Yeah, on a Saturday. Too early. I'm surprised you're even here."

"Why? Where else would I be?"

"I had a feeling you were going to sneak out to visit your booty call."

I wasn't intending on making his message common knowledge, but before I could try and hide it, Lauren had dropped me in it to Joe, announcing that I'd been summoned to Trey's bed.

"Nope. I told you, I'm done. I need to focus on

my job. Plus, he's not exactly a forever kinda guy, and I think that's what I need. It's time I stopped messing about and thought about my future."

"Whoa, when did you grow up and get all sensible and shit?"

"Since now. I've pretended I'm eighteen for long enough. I want what Ben and Lauren have."

"Don't we all." I narrow my eyes at him, still concerned with how he's taking things after their fall out. I know she says she's forgiven him, but even I can see that she's not as open with him as she once was, and he's taking it harder than he'll ever admit. "Where are you off to?"

"Meeting Lauren for brunch. Wanna join?"

"Nah, I'm gonna have a couple of strong coffees and then hit the gym. If I'm lucky I'll find a gym bunny to spend the afternoon with."

"Do you ever think about anything other than sex?"

"Do you?" My face flames red as what I did last night fills my mind. "Exactly. Wish me luck."

Laughing, I pull the front door open and head out into the hall. I'm still a bit early for meeting Lauren, but seeing as the weather's nice, I figure I'll walk and make the most of trying to clear my head of all things Trey.

I'm walking down the stairs, looking at a message

that's just come through from my sister when I bump into a brick wall—or more so a hot and sweaty man chest.

"Shit, I'm so...oh fuck!"

"Erica?" he growls, sending heat racing to my centre.

"Uh..." I'm totally lost for words. He's standing before me with a pair of shorts hanging low on his hips, his sculpted chest and abs on full display and covered in a perfect sheen of sweat. His t-shirt is draped over one shoulder and his hair's wet and all over the place. But it's his eyes that really capture mine. They're dark. Darker than I've seen them before, and they hold a promise that has me squirming.

What was I just saying about forgetting about this man?

"I knew you couldn't fucking resist." In one quick move, he's got me over his shoulder, and together we're running up the stairs. His fingers dig into my arse as he holds me, my hair hanging over my head as I stare at the rippling of his back muscles every time he moves.

It's only minutes later that I hear the unlocking of a door and I'm sliding down his body.

"That sure was something special I had to wake up to this morning, sweetheart. I've been hard ever since. The sounds of you moaning are on constant repeat in my head." He reaches out for my wrist before placing my hand against his length. I can't help myself and I wrap my fingers around the width. "And I jerked off at least three times before going out."

"Trey," I whimper, my own body now trembling with need.

"It seems my reply had a similar effect. Are you ready to give in to me now?" My teeth sink into my bottom lip as I try to make sense of his words. "That's mine." He pops my lip free before slamming his down and sucking it into his mouth. He bites down and I squeal, but the pain only makes the throbbing of my pussy worse.

"You tease me and I'll tease right back, sweetheart. Now, I need what was promised to me."

"I didn't promise anything."

He doesn't respond. Instead he takes a step back, places his hands on my hips and spins me around. My face is pressed against the cushion on his sofa as he presses down on my back to bend me over the arm. With my arse in the air, I'm in the perfect position for him.

He flips my skirt up, the cool air rushing across my heated skin. His fingers grip the sides of my knickers and he tugs until the lace gives and they fall away from my body.

Kicking my feet wider, his fingers find my heated core and I moan like a whore when he presses them down on my clit.

"You really fucking liked that picture, didn't you?" I groan as he starts to circle my swollen clit. "Answer me, or I'll stop." Moisture floods my core at his demanding tone and a growl rumbles up his throat.

"Yes, yes. I loved it."

He rewards me by thrusting two fingers deep inside me. My muscles clamp around him, desperately trying to drag him deeper to hit the magic spot too.

"Greedy little bitch. You're not getting off until my cock's buried deep inside your pussy."

Holy fuck.

"Please," I moan, needing what he's just suggested right fucking now.

The rustle of fabric fills my ears before the heat of his cock presses against my clit and rubs down to my entrance.

"Trey." His name falls from my lips without me realising, a plea for him to stop teasing me and to give in to what we both need.

I don't have the chance to beg any more; his

restraint must snap. Finding my entrance, he slides all the way in in one quick thrust of his hips. My feet leave the floor, his fingers bruising my hips to stop me falling completely onto his sofa.

He doesn't give me much time to adjust before he's pulling back out and slamming into me once again. His thrusts come harder and faster, telling me that maybe I made the right decision in ignoring his demands last night if it's made him this desperate for me. His balls slap against my pussy and he circles his hips, ensuring he grazes that perfect spot deep inside me.

I cry out when his palm lands on my arse cheek, pushing me closer to falling over the edge into the mind-numbing pleasure I so desperately need.

My orgasm is about to crash into me when my phone starts ringing.

"Leave it."

I panic and tense. No one ever rings me, which has me on high alert in case there's a problem.

"I need—"

"I said leave it."

Any argument I might have dies on my tongue as he grinds his hips into me. His movement reawakens my orgasm, and with only one more thrust I cry out his name as I fall over the edge. My body shakes, my muscles tensing as he continues to pound into me, desperately trying to find his own release.

I'm just coming down from my high, my body getting heavy and melding itself into the sofa cushions, when his cock swells, filling me even more than before. His roar bounces off the walls around us before his twitches inside me and the feeling of his hot cum filling me has me on the verge of another release.

"Fucking hell," he pants, folding over my back and resting his forehead against my shoulder. He's only there a few seconds before he stands and pulls out of me.

Pushing my exhausted body from his sofa, I turn to look at him. His hair's sticking up in all directions, his cheeks are pink from exertion and his lips swollen. I'm hit with a need so strong to walk into his arms that I reach down for where my bag fell on the floor when we entered and run for his front door.

"Thanks for that. It was...fun."

Throwing the door open, I run for the stairs, hoping like hell that he's not going to chase me because I'm not sure I have it in me to deny him what he so clearly wants right now.

There's a taxi idling across the street. I don't give a fuck if he's waiting for someone; I jump in the back and demand he takes me away right this second. He opens his mouth to argue but takes one look at the state of me and floors it. He probably thinks I'm trying to escape from a mad man or something, although as I sit back and think about it, it's not that far from the truth.

"Just here's fine. Thank you so, so much." I hand over more money than the journey was worth and hop out, knowing I'm a safe distance from our building now.

My shaky legs just about carry me to the wall, where I lean back against it and desperately try to suck in some much needed air.

I can't believe I just did that.

The image of him with his semi-hard dick hanging out as he watched me run for the door fills my mind. I try to fight down the little voice inside my head that's screaming for me to go back.

I did the right thing, I did the right thing, I repeat over and over again.

I probably look like a crazy person on the street right now, but I tell myself that this is London, and there are much odder people around than me.

My phone rings in my bag and it's only then that I remember it going off earlier. I rush to pull it out and breathe a sigh of relief when I see Lauren's name lighting up the screen.

"Hey, I'm sorry. I'm running a little late. I'm just around the corner."

"Okay. I'll wait to order then."

Attempting to smooth down my hair, I rub at my lips, knowing my lipstick is going to be all over my face. Trying to hold my head up high, I walk towards the café my best friend is sitting in. I need her level head right now.

CHAPTER TEN

"WHAT HAPPENED TO YOU?" Lauren asks the second I step up to the table.

"Trey happened."

"Couldn't resist then, huh? Temptation just too close to handle?"

Dropping down into the seat opposite her, I grab the menu and quickly make a decision before the waitress comes over. Lauren's stare burns into the top of my head the whole time.

It's not until the waitress has been and gone that she says any more. "So...didn't care to mention that you lived in the same building?"

"I was trying to ignore it. He's been stomping around above my head, taunting me, daring me to go up since the first night I met him. It's been torture."

"So why didn't you just do it?"

"I don't need a man, Lauren."

"I know, you keep saying. But, honestly, none of us *need* a man, E. Life would probably be a hell of a lot easier without one, but sometimes they're impossible to ignore. Especially when they're stomping around above your head."

"This is a fucking nightmare," I moan, dropping my head into my hands.

"Yeah, finding a hot man who's crazy about you... there's nothing worse than that."

"Don't, please. I need you to tell me that this is a bad idea. That he's going to break my heart like all the others and leave me with nothing. I'm already getting too attached, and I haven't allowed him in at all."

"You don't know any of that. Yeah, it could end in disaster but it also could be the best decision you ever make."

"I don't need to hear this," I mutter, making her laugh.

"Oh, come on. Where's the happy-go-lucky Erica who's up for anything? You used to be all about seeing where the ride took you and embracing the bumps along the way."

"She's been burned one too many times."

"You're going to allow Matt and my dad of all people to stop you from taking a chance? They were both arseholes. You can't let what happened with them stop you from living."

"What happened to you? I liked it better when you were heartbroken and hated men with a passion."

"Sorry, my heart was put back together again. Proof that happiness is out there. You just need to put your heart on the line sometimes. I told every single one of you to do anything in your power to keep me away from Ben when he first returned, but look how that turned out. There's no way I'm going to stop you doing something that might turn out to be the epic love story you crave."

"Who says I crave an epic love story?"

Her eyebrow lifts as she sits back in her chair and studies me. "Who doesn't?"

Our conversation slows as our meals arrive, but I can sense Lauren's stare every time she looks up at me.

"So tell me," I say, pushing my plate away and sitting back. "What do you think I should do?"

"I think you need to put the past behind you, forgive yourself for what happened and allow yourself a chance at happiness." Her words sound so simple, so why does even the thought of giving him a chance have my stomach tied up in knots?

"What if it's not that simple?"

"I never said it was going to be simple. You've been let down by men your entire life, I understand that. But he might be the one."

"Or he might be another one to let me down."

"Only one way to find out. Now come on, I want details from this morning. You turned up looking like you'd been fucked six ways from Sunday."

"I literally bumped into him coming back from a run as I headed down the stairs to come and meet you."

"What did he think you were doing there?"

"Following orders." Her brows pinch, so I tell her about the message exchanges we've had.

"Okay, that's kinda hot. But he still has no idea you live only a floor beneath him?"

"Not that I know of. And I'd like to keep it that way, if that's okay with you."

"Don't you think being honest might be the best way to start whatever this thing between you is?"

"And have him turning up whenever he wants, making crazy demands? No."

"Crazy demands...hot and sexy demands..." she trails off with a laugh. "Seriously though, just take it one day at a time. If he deserves your trust, he's going to have to earn it. You've been burned; he'll understand. That could be one of the benefits of an older man. Nothing wrong with a little life experience."

"Why do you have to be so level-headed?"

"Because it's happening to you. You know for a fact that I was nowhere near level-headed while Ben and I were trying to get our shit together."

"True story. More coffee?"

"Yes."

THE REST of my weekend is pretty much as it usually is, aside from the tempting footsteps from the man above my head. Joe tries to convince me to go out with him on Saturday night, but I point blank refuse to change out of my pyjamas and move off the sofa. His face was filled with disappointment, but he didn't push me on it. I think he thought I was lying and had plans with Trey. I feel guilty enough that I haven't told him Trey is actually our neighbour, so if I did have plans with him I would have owned up.

In reality, I haven't heard from Trey since I ran away from him on Saturday morning.

I expected to have had a call or at least a message, but it's been radio silence. It makes me wonder if he's happy now because he got what he needed and he's forgotten about me. I wish I could say that were true for me. Not a second's passed since leaving his flat in which I've managed to get him out of my mind.

As always, I meet my sister for our weekly yoga class on Sunday morning before heading to see Mum. It's been our routine for years now, and it's the one thing I can rely on staying the same as the rest of my life has spiralled out of control. My older sister, Samantha, has the life I crave. She's engaged to a guy who looks at her like she's his entire reason for being. He wasn't her first love, and knowing that does give me a little hope for myself. There was a time when I thought we were both too screwed up from our childhood to find a real, meaningful relationship, but thankfully she's proving me wrong. They're due to get married in a few weeks in an intimate wedding I've helped her plan. I'm looking forward to walking her down the aisle in her gorgeous white dress, but at the same time a part of me feels like she's moving on. She's been such a huge part of my life, especially during my teenage years. I know I'm being selfish, wanting to keep her to myself, but she's been my rock my entire life and I fear what I'll do if she—rightly so—moves on to have her own family.

Having fallen asleep embarrassingly early last night, I'm up at the crack of dawn and, without much else to do, I head for the office early. I expect it to still be in darkness, but, as I approach, the light from Ben's office shines brightly through the window.

A familiar voice fills my ears and a shiver runs down my spine. I don't need to hear the words he's saying; the deep timbre of his voice is enough to affect me.

"Just give her some time and a little space if she needs it. Don't be like all the other men who've been in her life."

"What does that mean?"

"Not my story to tell, man. If Erica wants you to know, she'll have to tell you herself."

My heart pounds as I listen to them talk about me. How fucking dare they? Racing forward, I push on Ben's office door so hard that it swings open and crashes back against the newly plastered wall.

"Have you two just about finished?" I snap, my eyes wide and my brows almost meeting my hairline. "You want to know something about me?" I bark, stepping closer to Trey and poking him in the chest with my index finger. "Fucking ask me. And you," I say turning my heated stare to Ben, "stay out of it. This is my life, and if I don't want to be screwing another member of this firm then I think I have a bloody good enough reason not to, wouldn't you say?" My eyes narrow at Ben and he swallows. I doubt he's scared of me; I think the only person he's scared of is Lauren, but he puts on a good show.

"I was just trying to help," he admits.

"Well, don't. I'm more than capable of looking after myself. I've damn well been doing it long enough."

Tears burn the backs of my eyes. In fear of them spilling over and showing Trey just how much of an emotional mess I really am, I turn my back on them and storm from the office.

No words are said as I make my way to the kitchen and slam the door behind me. Turning the kettle on, I allow the sob I'm fighting to keep down to break free. My eyes pool with water and, before long, tears spill down onto my cheeks.

Fuck them. Fuck all of them, I want to scream as I slam my hand down on the counter, embracing the sting of pain.

I've always been the strong one. I've never allowed anyone on the outside to see what my world was really like, to see the pain that festered inside from all the let downs and betrayals I've endured. What I don't need is for someone else, best friend or not, to be telling Trey what it is I do or do not need.

I am the one in control here. If he has problems, he needs to address me, not go behind my back.

My head's hanging between my shoulders with

my palms resting on the counter when the click of the lock drags me from my nightmare. I don't look up. I don't move in the hope that whoever it is will just leave me the hell alone.

Unfortunately, that's not Ben's style. It never has been. Other than my sister, he's the only other person who really gets me, who understands what it's like. I think I knew that from the first day I looked into his eyes. They held the same shadows, the loss, the pain. He knew, and without speaking a word about what either of us had been through, it was like we just gravitated towards each other. Our shared pain was strong enough to bond us together without even understanding it. It's why it hurt so damn much when he joined the other waste-of-space men in my life and upped and left without so much as a fucking warning. Now he's back, and I have first-hand experience of what happened to make him leave. I understand his intentions, but that doesn't mean the bitter sting of being abandoned once again by someone who was meant to love me isn't still buried within me.

His warm hand wraps around my shoulder and I'm twisted around until I'm pressed up against his solid chest. His strong arms wrap around me, and I'm powerless to do anything but soak up his support and cry into his chest.

"I'm sorry, E. I wasn't trying to go behind your back or tell him anything that isn't my place to tell. I was just trying to help. To stop him being quite so full-on. I know that—"

"Enough," I whisper. Even my voice sounds broken. "It's okay. I'm sorry."

I trust Ben one hundred percent with my secrets, but that doesn't mean that what I just overheard doesn't sting, even if I know he has my best interests at heart.

Once my breathing's calmed, Ben pushes on my shoulders and moves me back slightly so he can look into my eyes.

"I know you better than you think I do, and I can tell that you're freaking out right now. You like him, that much is obvious, but you're scared—and I understand why. I can see how intense he is, and I know that's pushing you away. I was just trying to allow you a little breathing space."

Wiping the tears staining my cheeks with the back of my hand, I look up into his blue eyes and can't help but smile. My heart aches with his need to try to protect me, and I love him just that little bit more for it.

"Thank you, I do appreciate it. Things between us are..."

"Explosive?"

"Ha, yeah, you could say that. But I have no intentions on whatever it is continuing. I've screwed up here enough already. You're drowning in debt because of my last mistake. The best thing for me to do is walk away before I screw something else up for you."

"And what if you don't."

"Jesus, you sound just like Lauren," I mutter, going over to the coffee machine. If we're going to have this kind if serious conversation then I need more caffeine.

"I must be rubbing off on her."

I snort, almost dropping coffee everywhere. "I'm sure you are, boss."

"As often as I can," he says with a cheeky wink. "But that's not what I meant. Just trust us, we know what we're talking about."

"Doubtful."

"Careful. I am your boss, you know?"

"Like you're going to let me forget it."

"We good now, yeah?" He glances towards the door, probably ready to escape my emotional breakdown.

"Yeah, we're good."

"All right, well, I don't pay you to make coffee."

"Sure thing, boss." I salute him and he pulls the door open, his shoulders shaking with a laugh.

I sit down at my desk, no less confused about Trey, but after my little chat with Ben I do feel a little lighter.

After taking a cautious sip of coffee, I turn my computer on and drag my diary to the centre of the desk. Flipping it open, I stare down at what's first on my list today, but I don't get that far because written across every single day past the five o'clock line in huge bold Sharpie letters is 'TREY'.

My teeth grind as fire ignites in my veins. See, this is one reason you should never sleep with a colleague: they think it gives them the right to mess with your work day.

"Where is he?" I bark. Seeing as we're still the only two in the office, it should be obvious who I'm talking to and about.

"Gone to site. Why, you need something only he can give?"

"Fuck off." He can't see me, but I flip him off anyway.

CHAPTER ELEVEN

I MANAGED to escape early Monday afternoon, and Tuesday he ended up stuck in a meeting so I was able to sneak off home without being caught, but I know my time avoiding him is coming to an end...and that's not just because every message and email I receive from him tells me so.

Stepping out of the office on Wednesday afternoon ready for a trip to the post office with a load of letters, I sigh in frustration when I discover the rain is harder than I was expecting. Pulling my umbrella from my bag, I'm just about to step out into the torrential downpour when a car pulls into the driveway.

Even from this distance, I see his eyes light up and a smug smile twitch at his lips. I attempt to walk past him with my head held high, but his window is down by the time I get to him.

"Get in," he demands.

"I'm good, thanks."

"Erica." His deep, gravelly voice hits me right between the legs. "You're getting wet."

"It's fine. I quite like it." His eyes glisten in delight, and I chastise myself for egging him on.

"I can put an end to that. Get in."

"I'm sure you've got plenty of work to do." I take another step, but his arm flies out and grabs mine.

"Nothing that's more important than you."

I look back at him. Our eyes meet and my resolve to stay away from him weakens.

"Fine, just drop me at the post office. It's right next to the tube station for me to get home."

"Just get in."

Following orders this time, I quickly make my way around to the passenger door and slide in once I've closed my umbrella.

"See, it wasn't that hard, was it?"

The second I shut the door, the tension between us makes it hard to breathe. The last time I was alone with him, I was bent over the arm of his sofa.

"So..." I say, tapping my hand against my thigh, not really knowing if I should be making small talk or what.

"Why'd you run?"

My head snaps over to his, my eyes wide with shock that he's diving straight into the issue.

"I...uh...got what I came for?" I don't mean it to come out as a question, but the squeak in my voice makes it sound that way.

"You really expect me to believe you made the effort to come to my flat just for that?"

"Of course. That's what a booty call is, right?"

"If you say so."

Silence descends, but it's only a few moments later when he's pulling into a parking spot right out the front of the post office.

"Thank you for the ride."

"You're more than welcome. I'm free for rides any day of the week." I try my best to ignore the innuendo, but it's easier said than done.

"I'll...uh...see you tomorrow. Thanks." Jumping from the car, I slam the door and run before he has the chance to say anything or stop me.

My heart pounds and my chest heaves like I've just run here as I stand in the queue, but that's the effect his mere presence has on me. One look at him and I'm just a ball of need. If it were true that a man could melt a woman's knickers, he'd be able to do it. Mine threaten to drop the second I look at him.

I try to convince myself that that's all it is, just a

physical attraction, but as much as I try to ignore it, I know it's more than that. When I'm around him, I have this unnerving need to spill all my dark secrets in the hope that he'll take the weight of them for me. I've never in my life felt like that about another person; even the few who know the truth about my life had to drag it out of me; with him, the words are ready to just fall from my lips.

It's that knowledge that makes me keep him at arm's length. Men before him have managed to break me without the power that comes with sharing my secrets. If I were to open up, when he screws me over it'll be even more earth-shattering.

Thankfully, the rain's slowed by the time I make it back outside. Keeping my head down, I turn towards the tube station—until a very familiar and very solid wall stops me in my tracks.

"Where are you going?" he growls, his hands on my upper arms, causing sparks to shoot around my body.

Dragging my eyes up his shirt-covered chest, I find his intense steel eyes staring down at me. "Home?"

"Let me take you."

"You...you waited so you could take me home?"

"Yeah. Why is that so hard to believe?" Reaching out, he runs a lock of my hair between his fingers. He obviously doesn't expect an answer, but to be fair, if he listened to anything Ben said on Monday morning then he already knows I'm not used to guys being so...nice. I'm used to following demands, taking orders and fending for myself. This...his genuine kindness is a little unnerving. "Wouldn't you rather be in my car than sitting on a sweaty tube?"

"Of course. What are you expecting in return?" My eyes narrow as I try to figure out his angle.

He leans in. I half expect him to kiss me, but at the last minute he turns his head to the side and whispers in my ear, "Have dinner with me?"

"Dinner?"

"Yeah, dinner. You say where and we'll go."

"And then what?"

"Whatever you want."

"You just want to have dinner? No funny business?"

"Like I said, whatever you want."

Standing to his full height, his eyes flit over my face. I've no idea if he finds what he was looking for or not, but he nods his head, runs his hand down my arm and locks his fingers with mine, pulling me back to his car.

Like a real gentleman, he opens the door for me and waits until I'm settled before he closes it and makes his way to the driver's side. I drag as much air into my lungs as possible, knowing that when he joins me and closes his door it's going to suck all the air out.

"So," he asks, turning to me once he's brought the engine to life. "What do you fancy?"

You is right on the end of my tongue, but I manage to bite it back. "A curry."

"Good choice. Any particular restaurant?"

"Nope, I don't have a favourite." The one my sister and I used to order from on a weekly basis closed down a little while after we both moved out of our family home. I've not managed to find one anywhere close to its quality since.

"Lucky for you, I do and it's incredible. It's a little out of the city, though—you okay to drive for a bit?"

I probably shouldn't allow myself to be locked in this enclosed space with him for any length of time, but the promise of an incredible curry is enough to have me agreeing and getting comfortable in his soft leather seat. "As long as it's as good as you say."

"I won't let you down." I know we're talking about a curry here, but something tells me he means more than that. Butterflies dance in my belly no matter how many times I tell myself not to fall for his charm.

He'll only break you, like all the others.

HIS INDIAN OF choice is a little back street restaurant. It doesn't look much from outside, and I probably would never have chosen it if I were walking past, but after descending some stairs the most incredible dining room is revealed. We're shown to our table in a quiet corner, and the waiter leaves us for a few minutes.

"So, tell me..." I look up at Trey curiously and try to ignore the racing of my heart as I wait for the end of his sentence. "Are you the kind of girl who always has the same dish, or do you like to try different things?"

Relieved he didn't demand something more personal, a smile spreads across my face. "You tell me. What do you think?"

"I think you try it all, and the more exotic the better."

"Hmmm..." I run my eyes over the menu in front of me. "I guess you'll never know."

"I don't intend on this being our one and only meal, Erica."

"It takes two to tango, Trey, which means you'd need me to agree to this not being our one and only meal."

"I have ways to convince you."

Heat floods my belly as his eyes darken with desire. "Is that right?" My voice is husky, giving away how he really makes me feel. Lifting the menu slightly, I attempt to hide behind it but all he does is laugh at me. I fear I'm never going to be able hide from him.

The whole evening is incredible...Trey is incredible. He's thoughtful, caring, and a total gentleman. I'm afraid that I'm beginning to like him a little too much. I don't have the strength right now to have my heart smashed to pieces, but I'm having a hard time keeping it out of what's developing between us.

"Thank you so much for the meal," I say as he leads us from the restaurant, his hand tightly wrapped around mine.

"You're welcome."

He holds the car door open for me once again and helps me inside. The second he shuts the door, loneliness settles within me. It's crazy, because he's just walking around the car to get in, but knowing I'm starting to rely on how he makes me feel is unsettling.

After dropping into the driver's seat, he turns to look at me.

"What?" I ask, starting to feel a little self-conscious.

"I've no idea where you live. Point me in the right direction."

The truth is on the tip of my tongue, but a bigger part of me is scared to allow him into my life more than he already is, so, when I open my mouth, another address entirely falls from my lips.

The drive is quiet, and it makes me nervous. He's being so sweet. I know he listened to Ben's warning the other day and is trying to be more than the demanding lover I've known up until this point, but, quite honestly, he was easier to deal with like that.

I knew what he wanted, and I could give him what he needed.

Whatever this is, this getting to know each other...it scares me. If he gets to know me, that means I've allowed him in, and that gives him power.

It gives him the power to break me, and I promised myself I'd never give anyone that kind of power over me again. I can only pick myself up so many times, and I'm not sure I'd survive the level of heartache Trey could cause if I were to give him the chance.

Bringing the car to a stop, he pulls the handbrake and his stare burns into my skin.

"Thank you for a lovely evening."

He's silent for a few seconds. Thinking he's not

going to say any more, I undo the seat belt and put my hand on the handle.

"Spend the weekend with me," he blurts out.

"W-what?" I stutter.

His fingers twist with mine and he tugs my arm so I have no choice but to turn back towards him. His face is deadly serious and hope shines from his eyes.

"Spend the weekend with me. Get to know the real me. Let me show you who I am, prove that you can trust me."

"Uh..." My eyes run over every inch of his face, looking for any indication that he's joking, but I find nothing.

My heart hammers against my chest as I fight to drag in the air I need, but it's like someone's suddenly sucked it all out of the car.

"I...uh...I need to go." He allows me to pull my hand from his and, as quickly as I can, I jump from the car and practically run towards the building. His eyes don't leave me the entire way to the front door, but I don't dare turn around. Instead, I pull the keys from the bottom of my bag and let myself into the ground floor flat.

"Hello?" my sister shouts, sounding a little panicked from the living room.

"It's just me."

Samantha pops her head around the doorframe,

concern etched into every one of her features. "What's happened?"

"You got any wine?"

"You know it. Come on."

I follow behind her towards her kitchen, stopping on the way to say hello to her fiancé.

I sit at her small dining table as she pulls a bottle from the fridge and fills two glasses.

"So, tell me about him."

"How do you know there's a him?" She lifts a brow but doesn't say anything. "Okay, fine. Yeah, there's a him."

"I'm waiting."

"I hooked up with this guy a couple of weeks ago. Totally my type. He's—"

"An arsehole?"

"What?" My brows pinch together.

"Oh come on, Erica. We both know exactly what your type is. You've got this natural ability to pick out the utter scumbags every single time. How is this guy any different?"

My sudden need to defend Trey to my sister freaks me out. I don't really know him, so he could very well be as bad as all the others, even if deep down I really want to believe he's different.

"Anyway, he turned up at work. He's our new contracts manager."

A laugh falls from her lips. "You're kidding, right?"

"I wish."

"Jesus, Erica. How do you end up in these situations?"

"Fucked if I know."

"So now what? You've been with him again, I assume?"

My face heats. "He just took me out for dinner and asked me to spend the weekend with him."

"Okay. So...why are you here?"

"He wanted to take me home, but I gave him your address instead."

"Why?" she asks, confusion written all over her face.

I pause briefly, wondering if I should tell her the truth. In the end, I do with a half-truth. "I don't want him getting too close."

"So he thinks you live here?"

"I guess so."

"What did you say about the weekend?"

"I didn't. I ran."

"Fucking hell, Erica."

CHAPTER TWELVE

ALTHOUGH TREY HASN'T SAID anything about the weekend, I can see the question written all over his face every time he looks at me. I hate it. I've no idea what I should do. I hate everything right now. I hate that he seems to be giving me the space that I thought I needed, and I hate that he's no longer the demanding lover that he was at the beginning. I fear he's softening, and fuck if it wasn't his demanding attitude that made him so damn irresistible in the first place.

It's just after lunchtime when he disappears out of the office for a site visit, and I pull my phone from my bag. Seeing a missed call from my sister hours ago, I return it straight away.

"I've got something pretty impressive for you."

"Sorry, I'm not into chicks," I say with a laugh. If

it were Trey's deep voice saying those words, I'd damn near lose my shit.

"Ha, you're funny. Has lover boy said anything to you?"

"Not really, he's been pretty quiet actually. Why?"

"Because I've got the biggest bunch of flowers I think I've ever seen sitting in my living room, and they've got your name on them."

"Shut the fuck up. You're joking, right?"

"Nope. You need to come and get them before Cliff starts thinking I'm having an affair weeks before our wedding."

"He'd never think that, but I'll stop by after work."

"I'm sending you a picture now. You need to see them."

"Okay, see you later."

I've barely hung up when my phone vibrates with a picture.

"Fucking hell," I mutter to myself, my eyes widening in shock at the sheer number of flowers. Another picture comes through, and it's of the back of the card.

Trey: 10am Saturday morning. Pack a bag.

Excitement and fear hit my stomach, making it turn over. Spending the weekend with him is dangerous, but can I say no?

Before leaving for the day, I check the calendar. He's booked in for a meeting with Ben after work. Knowing he'll be coming back any minute, I make a rash decision.

Grabbing a Sharpie from the pen pot on his desk, I find tomorrow in his diary and write across it, much like he did in mine last week.

Erica: See you soon. E x

A bolt of excitement races through me and, before I can change my mind and rip the page from his diary, I run from the office.

"WHOA, WHO'D YOU PISS OFF?" Joe asks once I've fought my way into our flat with the giant arrangement of flowers I picked up from my sister's.

"I love how you think I must have annoyed someone to receive something like this," I sulk, dropping them to the kitchen counter and shaking out my arms.

"Why else would someone...wait? Do not tell me Trey sent them?"

"What do you think?"

"I think he's not the kind of guy to do romantic shit like that." He plucks the card from the middle and flips it over. "Ha, see. It's just a fancy booty call. You really spending the weekend with him?"

"Yes. No. Maybe." The whole way home, I regretted pretty much agreeing to it, although I've no way of knowing if he's seen my note.

"Want to come out for a drink to help you decide?"

"Nah, I think I'll stay in, have a bath or something."

"Erica Wilde refusing a drink on a Friday night. What is happening right now?"

"Oh shut up. It's not that unusual." His raised eyebrow tells me that it really is, but I ignore it. I need to decide what I'm going to do, and going out and getting drunk is not going to help making a rational decision.

"Oh wait...you're going to spend the night pruning, ready for your hot weekend, aren't you?" His eyes drop between my legs inquisitively.

"Nope. That's already been taken care of, thank you very much."

"I'm sure he'll appreciate that. Well, if you're

being a boring bitch, I think I'll leave you to it."

"Have fun," I call when he gets to the front door. "And if you bring someone home, make sure they're quiet."

"You'd better hope I bring someone home, otherwise I'll be coming after you, it's been so fucking long."

Laughing at him, I wish him luck and watch him disappear.

I spend the entire night trying to decide if I should pack a bag or not. My body says 'fuck yes'; it's begging for that amount of one-on-one time with Trey, but my head is screaming something very different. I just don't know which one is shouting louder, and I can't deny that what my body wants is so fucking tempting.

***

I WAKE LATER than I was expecting the next morning, after a fitful night's sleep full of indecision and dirty dreams. The second I swing my legs off the side of the bed, I know what I need to do.

Dragging my suitcase from the top of my wardrobe, I make quick work of stuffing everything I might need inside before having a very quick shower, curling my hair, applying my make-up and sliding my favourite dress up my body. I want to look sexy without looking like I've put too much effort into it.

After sending my sister a text so she's expecting me, I make myself a coffee in my travel mug and set off. I'm already running a little late. The last thing I want is for him to think I decided against his offer after all of this.

I'm a nervous wreck by the time the taxi pulls up outside my sister's house. My palms are sweating and I swear a zoo full of fucking butterflies have taken up residence in my stomach. The journey took longer than it usually would, thanks to some festival in the local park.

"You look like you're about to puke," my sister helpfully points out when she lets me in.

"I need to pee."

Her laughter follows me down to her bathroom, where I have another nervous wee before joining her in the living room. I sit on the chair in front of the window so I can see the second he pulls up.

"I'm not sure I've ever seen you so unsure of yourself."

"Not helping," I mutter, my eyes glued to the window.

"I know I've not met this guy, but something tells me he's different."

Now that gets my attention. "Different how?"

"*You're* different. Although you're nervous as shit right now, I can't help feeling like something's settled inside you."

Narrowing my eyes at her cryptic statement, I turn back to the window. "That's all well and good, whatever it's meant to mean, but where the hell is he? It's almost ten past."

"I'm sure he's coming. You said yourself that the traffic was bad."

Blowing out a slow breath, I tell myself that she's right. He'll be here.

By twenty past ten, I'm starting to lose my shit. I spent all night worrying about this and he hasn't even bothered to show his face. *Was it all one big joke?*

"Has he tried ringing? Where's your phone?"

Pulling my bag from the floor, I slide my hand into the pocket where it lives. Empty. *Shit.* Rummaging through each pocket, my heart starts to race.

"I can't find it."

Dropping to my knees, I open my little suitcase and start pulling everything out in case it got tangled in something.

"Shit, shit, shit." Huffing out a frustrated breath, I try to think of when I last had it while surrounded by the contents of my case. "It's next to the fucking coffee machine."

"He's probably rung to say he's running late or something. Just chill, yeah?"

"Yeah," I agree although I feel anything but chilled right now.

I'm just about to start stuffing everything back into my case when the buzzer rings loudly throughout the flat. My eyes widen in panic as I look at Sam, who's moving to look out the window.

"It's him. I'll go—"

"No," I whisper-shout. "Do not open the door."

"Why?"

"He still thinks I live here."

Shaking her head at me, my sister drops to her knees to help me collect up all my stuff and attempt to get it back inside my case. "You do know you're only going for one night, right?" she asks, counting the number of knickers I flung across her living room.

"You never know how many you'll need on a dirty weekend."

"TMI, lil' sis." I can't help but laugh at the horrified look on her face—that is, until the buzzer goes off again.

"Shit."

"Go fucking answer it, then."

"Okay, okay." Smoothing down my hair, I wheel my case out into the hallway. "Hide!" Sam puts her hands up in defeat and backs into the room, out of sight.

I take a second to attempt to compose myself, but after the last ten minutes I think it might be a lost cause.

I flick the lock but don't get a chance to pull the door open because it's done for me. He takes one look at me and steps a little closer, concern filling his steel eyes.

"What's wrong?"

My forehead wrinkles. "Nothing, why?"

"I've been trying to call you, and you look at bit harassed."

"I'm fine. I left my phone at..." I trail off just in time to catch myself before I admit that I don't live here. "At Joe's."

A noise from behind me forces me to look over my shoulder. All I can do is roll my eyes at my sister who's still hidden from Trey, but I can clearly see her alternating between fanning herself and putting her thumbs up.

"As long as you're okay." When I look back, his eyes are following mine.

"I'm really good. Shall we go?" Placing my hand on his chest, his eyes immediately come back to me, darkening as our gaze holds for a few seconds. I'm beginning to get used to the sparks between us, and the butterflies that had settled in my stomach slightly take flight again.

"This bag?" he asks, nodding down to my little case.

"That's the one." Following him out, I stop to pull the door closed and find my sister making very inappropriate gestures at Trey's back. Flipping her off, I close the door and run to catch up with him.

"Where are we going?" I ask once we're settled and he's pulled away from the curb.

"It's a surprise."

"It's a kinky sex den, isn't it?" The deep laugh that fills the car warms me all the way to my toes. It tells me that I made the right decision in agreeing to spend time with him, although it also confirms that if —when—this goes south, it's going to hurt like hell.

<hr>

"I ALWAYS THOUGHT these places would be in a basement or some old warehouse in the middle of no here," I say when he pulls down a long driveway with only grass and fields as far as I can see.

"I'm sure they probably are. I wouldn't know, I've not been."

"I'm not sure if I'm relieved or disappointed," I admit with a laugh. "Holy shit." My breath catches as we hit the top of the small hill we were climbing and the hotel he's brought us to is revealed.

"Stunning, isn't it?"

"It's...it's really something."

"What's wrong? Don't you like it?" He pulls the car to a stop and turns towards me. My eyes stay on the grand building in front of us, afraid to look his way and exposing my anxiety.

"I...uh...I don't fit in in a place like this. I don't have the kind of money these people do or own the kind of clothes they wear. I'm just not—"

"Erica," he interrupts. His warm fingers brush across my cheek, and I'm forced to turn to look at him, although I keep my eyes downcast. "Look at me." I follow his demand like always and meet his hard eyes. "You're already the most beautiful woman staying in this hotel. I don't even need to get out of the car to know that. You don't need money or designer clothes to fit in in a place like this. You just need to have confidence. I know you have plenty—it's one of the things I find so sexy about you. Hold your head up high, because I can guarantee that every man in that place is going to be jealous that you're here with me and sleeping in my bed tonight."

Tears burn, but I refuse to allow them to fill my eyes. I won't allow him to see my vulnerability and insecurities.

"Okay. Lead the way."

With his hand possessively in the small of my back, he walks us towards the entrance. The huge white building is by far the fanciest I've ever been in, let alone stayed in.

"Good morning, how can I help you?" The receptionist gives Trey her megawatt smile, and I can't help but step a little closer to him when her eyes drop to check him out. It's a move that doesn't go unnoticed by him, and he drops a kiss to the top of my head to really nail the point home.

"We have a room booked under Bennett."

She taps away on her keys before producing a key and pointing us in the direction of our room.

"It's on the top floor?" I ask when he presses the button in the lift.

"It is, and it's nothing less than you deserve." My blush heats my cheeks and spreads down my neck. I've never in my life been treated like this, and I've no idea how to take it.

"I've never stayed in a place like this before. No one's ever taken me anywhere, in fact." The words are out of my mouth before I realise I said them aloud.

As he turns to me, the intensity in his eyes forces me to take a step back until I bump into the handrail.

"Then it's time I showed you how you should be

treated." His hand wraps around the back of my neck and I'm powerless but to move towards his lips when his head dips. His lips brush mine in the gentlest of kisses, so alien to the harsh and dominant ones I've experienced from him before.

My heart races and my skin tingles with the need for more. Unfortunately, when the lift announces our arrival, all he does is take my hand and lead me out.

The room he takes me to is beyond my wildest dreams. It's got the biggest bed I've ever seen, covered in the most luxurious gold and cream sheets. All the furniture is huge and made of solid wood, but the space is so big that they almost look too small. The best bit is the french doors which lead to a balcony that looks out over the grounds.

"I think I might move in," I say, spinning around, trying to take it all in.

"You might need to win the lottery first." His mention of how much this might have cost has guilt sitting heavy in my stomach. "Don't," he warns, walking over and taking my cheeks in his hands. "Don't even think about it. Trust me when I say that if I didn't want this, I wouldn't have done it. I only ever do things because *I* want to. So don't be feeling guilty or any of that shit. Just relax and enjoy what I have planned."

"And what do you have planned?" My eyes flick over to the bed behind me and he chuckles.

"You'll have to wait and see, but right now, there should be a chilled bottle of champagne waiting for us on the balcony. Join me?"

He holds his hand out and I've no choice but to slide mine into it and follow him out. He's right, of course. Tucked beside the giant outdoor sofa is a chrome wine cooler with one very expensive bottle of bubbles inside. He lifts the blanket that's waiting for us and gestures for me to sit.

Dropping down, I allow the early winter sun to warm my skin and watch with delight as Trey pulls the bottle from the ice and sets about popping the top. The muscles of his exposed forearms strain, and an ache starts up low in my belly.

"The view's really quite incredible, right?" His eyes are locked on the scenery beyond, but I'm convinced he must be able to feel my hungry stare.

"Sure is." Turning back towards me, his eyes are dark, the muscle in his neck pulsating. Starting at my eyes, he drops his gaze down, taking in every inch of my body and running over the exposed skin of my thighs before finding my boots.

My body heats, my core throbbing to feel his hands on me. But instead of acting out any of the fantasies currently running rampant in my mind, he just hands me a glass of champagne before holding his out.

"To us."

"To us." My voice is barely more than a breathy whisper, and I swear his eyes get even darker. He knows exactly what I want, and it's frustrating the hell out of me that he's not taking what I'm so clearly desperate for.

"Drink up. We've got plans."

TWO HOURS LATER, I find myself in the building's basement wrapped in the thickest, softest white robe I've ever touched, having just had the most relaxing facial. Stepping out from the treatment room, I find Trey dressed exactly the same and resting back in a chaise longue with another glass of bubbles.

"Fancy seeing you here." His eyes snap up to mine before dropping to my exposed legs.

I fall down beside him. He hands me a glass and then takes my hand, tangling his fingers with mine.

"Thank you for all this. It's...incredible."

"It's about to get better."

"Really?" Biting down on my bottom lip, I think about what would make this experience complete, but when my dirty thoughts are interrupted by a therapist, I realise that's not what's happening—not yet, anyway.

"It's time for your couple's massage. If you'd like to follow me."

I glance at Trey as he stands and pulls me up with him. As soon as I'm at full height, his free arm wraps around my waist, pulling me against him. His cheek brushes against mine, his day old stubble sending sparks shooting off around my body. "I promise it'll be so worth it."

I sag against him and he chuckles in my ear before stepping back and finding my hand. I feel lost without his body pressed up against mine, and that little warning about how much I'm enjoying him starts screaming at me once again.

My head spins as I walk towards him. I've only had two half glasses, but add that to the desire coursing through my body and my lack of breakfast and I guess the bubbles have gone straight to my head.

"You okay?" Trey asks, looking back when I sway slightly on my feet.

"Yeah, I'm good."

"We'll eat after this. Soak up some of that alcohol."

I nod and smile at him, hoping not to give away just how tipsy I'm feeling all of a sudden.

We're directed into a room very much like the one I had my facial in only minutes ago. It's filled with flickering scented candles, and soft, relaxing music filters through the air.

"If you would both like to get yourselves comfortable on the tables, my colleague and I will be back in a few minutes to get started. He smiles at both of us and quietly steps from the room.

"What are we sup—" My words stop as Trey drops his robe to the floor. My teeth sink into my bottom lip as my eyes trail over every inch of his exposed skin. *Do they have to come back in?*

"Yeah they do." His words make my eyes snap up to his. I had no idea I'd asked that question aloud and, from the amusement in his dark eyes, I'd say he's aware of that fact. "Hurry up. I don't want anyone else's eyes on more of you than totally necessary."

His words only touch on how demanding he can be, but they have the same effect. Heat pools between my legs and my breath picks up pace.

"Don't make me lock that door and take matters into my own hands."

Holy shit.

I'm a second away from begging that he does just that when there's a knock at the door.

"Two minutes," Trey calls out before stepping up to me. His fingers find the knot at my waist and, in one quick movement, it's undone and he's pushing the fabric from my shoulders.

It pools at my feet, leaving me totally naked. His eyes drop to my breasts and my nipples tighten almost painfully.

A low rumble of a moan escapes him, and I instantly get wetter for him. I'm about three seconds from begging him to touch me when he takes a step back and orders for me to lie on the bed as we were instructed.

It takes me a couple of seconds to get my body to function as it should, something I think Trey notices if his smug smirk is anything to go by as he lifts the towel and places it over my bare body, going over to do the same to himself.

My entire body is alive with desire. I tilt my head to the side and find that Trey's doing exactly the same and staring right at me. He might not be voicing his demands today like I've become used to, but his power and dominance ooze from his steel grey eyes and it makes my stomach tighten with anticipation.

Before long, there's another knock at the door, and after Trey calls out to say we're ready we're joined by two masseuses. One look at them and I breathe a sigh of relief when I notice the man walk over to Trey. I'm not sure how I'd have coped seeing another woman with her hands all over him. A wave of jealousy like I've never known washes through me, making my teeth clench and my muscles to lock up tight. The lady standing beside me says a few things and I agree, but I've no idea what she's talking about; I'm too busy watching the guy walking around Trey.

After a few seconds, her warm hands land on my left leg and I just about manage to contain a moan of pleasure as her nimble fingers press into the flesh. I've never had a professional massage before, and I already know from one touch alone that it's going to be incredible.

I intend on watching Trey, but it's not long until my eyes start getting heavy and I'm forced to put my head in the little hole it's intended for.

The masseuse makes her way up to my back and I lose the fight. The soft music and gentle touch are too much on top of last night's sleepless night.

My eyes fly open the moment his fingers touch me. Every single part of my body is aware of the difference, of the electric current that's always sparking between us.

"Relax," he orders. "It's my time to have some fun."

At hearing his demanding voice, my body melts back into the bed I've been sleeping on for the past however long as the wonderful lady behind me worked out all of my kinks.

I smirk.

Trey is one kink she'll have to work a lot harder to get rid of.

Cool air hits my skin as he lifts the towel from me and drops it to the floor.

"Hmmm," he moans before his palm drops to squeeze the fullness of my arse. My core tightens.

I gasp when the warmth of his breath tickles my ear. My entire body is on fire and waiting for him to do something.

"Do you like happy endings, Erica?"

"I...ahhh." He doesn't give me the chance to answer properly because his fingers trail down my arse, he teases the puckered hole before dropping lower until he finds my entrance.

"So wet," he murmurs, his finger circling and driving me crazy for more.

"Please, Trey. Please," I beg, lifting my hips from the bed and trying to force him deeper. "I need...I need..."

"I know exactly what you need. And you'll get it...eventually." His lips start at the base of my neck and trail down my spine, causing goose-bumps in their wake. "I need to taste you," he admits when his lips hit the fullness of my behind.

His hands grip my hips and I squeal as he effortlessly flips me over. Shifting to the end of the bed, his fingers wrap around my ankles and I'm pulled down until I'm hanging over the edge. He drops to his knees and places my feet on his shoulders while pushing his hands on the inside of my thighs and opening me for him.

"Beautiful." My cheeks heat at knowing he's studying my pussy quite so intently. Propping myself up on my elbows, I look down at him. His eyes flick up to mine and the desire in them almost has me crashing back to the bed. I do exactly that the moment he leans forward and licks up the length of me.

"Fuck."

Pressing my legs even wider, he licks at me until my entire body is trembling with the need for him to push me over the edge, but every time I so much as get close he pulls back.

"Yes," I cry. This is exactly what I've needed since the moment he pushed the door open at my sister's. I need him to give me everything he's got. "Trey, please." My heart races and I have to fight to drag in the air I need as my focus is solely on the orgasm that's imminently going to crash through me.

Two thick fingers press into me. It's almost enough to have me flying, but he stills before sliding deeper, stopping me from falling over the edge. Not once does his tongue stop lapping at me—not that he can go far with my fingers twisted in his hair, holding him against me.

The second his fingers are as deep as they'll go, he bends them and hits my G-spot without any effort. It's like he knows my body almost as well as he does his own.

Every muscle in my body tightens, ruining all that woman's work before I snap. Lights flash behind my eyes and my body trembles as an earth-shattering release races through me. Trey's movements don't falter, ensuring I ride out every pleasurable second.

Once it subsides and my pussy stops clenching around him, he pulls back and out, lifting his fingers to his lips and sucking them into his mouth. His eyes roll back as he tastes me on himself. Little after-shocks flutter in my core, just watching him. I'm so ready for more, but unfortunately, once he's done, he stands and grabs his robe. His cock bobs, rock hard in front of him, but he refuses any offer I make to return the favour. It confuses and frustrates me in equal measures because it's obvious he needs it, but he won't allow himself the pleasure. Instead, he takes my hand and takes me back up to our room to get ready for dinner.

CHAPTER THIRTEEN

I SHOWER ALONE after Trey point-blank refused my offer to him of joining me, even though desire still filled his eyes and his cock was still tenting his robe.

I tried to fight the ball of emotion clogging my throat as I showered, but the more I tried to rid myself of it the stronger it became, until I found myself sobbing, hoping to get it all out while I was alone.

I take a long time getting ready. I fear what I might find on the other side of the door when I eventually pull it open. Has he changed his mind about me? Is he regretting bringing me here?

By the time my hair and make-up are done, I feel a little stronger. I tell myself that he isn't the kind of man to do anything he doesn't want to, so if he no longer wanted me here then I've no doubt he'd tell me and send me on my way. Blowing out a long breath, I wrap my fingers around the handle and pull it open. He's standing by the balcony, already dressed in a pair of black trousers and a perfectly pressed white shirt, despite the fact it's been packed in his bag for most of the day.

He hears me coming and turns to look over his shoulder. His eyes widen before they dilate. He turns his entire body my way as his eyes drop from mine to take in my body. He still wants me, that much is clear, so why won't he give me what I need?

My body heats as he takes in the trusty little black dress I shoved in my case, not knowing where we were going or what I'd need.

"You look beautiful." Walking over, he reaches for my hand and pulls it to his lips so he can kiss my knuckles. The gentlemanly move has my earlier emotion threatening to climb back up my throat.

"You're looking pretty sharp yourself."

"I'm nothing in comparison to you. Everyone is going to wonder why you're here spending time with me."

"Shut up, no they won't. They'll all be aware that you're my sugar daddy." It's meant to be a joke, but the way it comes out makes it sound anything but.

"That is not what this is," Trey says forcefully. His hand wraps around the back of my neck, his fingers twisting in the hair there, and his forehead drops to mine. "I really like you, Erica." His eyes bore into mine as my heart starts to race.

"I—"

"Shhh." His fingers press against my lips. "You don't need to say anything. Just let me prove to you that I'm worthy."

My forehead wrinkles. It's not the first time he's said that, and it makes me wonder what he knows about me—or what he thinks he knows. Neither option makes me happy.

"Are you hungry?"

"Ravenous." I hold back that the thing I'm ravenous for is him, because with my nipples pressing against the fabric of my dress and my increased breaths, I'd like to think he's already aware. What he gave me earlier in the therapy room only took the edge off. What I really need is him, all of him, and soon.

"Yeah," he chuckles, "I'm starving, too." His eyes drop from mine in favour of my lips, but he doesn't move to kiss them. "Come on." Pulling back, he takes my hand once again and pulls me towards the door. I want to stomp my foot like a child and demand he give me what we both so badly need, but, wanting to look like the mature and in control adult I am, I refrain and instead follow his lead.

We're shown to a secluded table in the back of the restaurant and Trey orders us a fancy bottle of champagne before we silently choose what we'd like to eat. My stomach summersaults with the confusion that's running rampant in my head, and I struggle to find the desire to eat anything, but when the waiter comes back I give him my order, hoping I look excited about it.

Trey eyes me curiously across the table. He sits back and studies me for a few seconds once we're alone again, sipping on his drink, deep in thought.

"Tell me, how'd you end up at Johnson & Sons? You don't seem the kind of girl who's always wanted a career in construction."

Taking a sip at my own drink, I consider how much I want to reveal about my life. "I'd dropped out of uni and needed a job. I sent out about a million CV's and they were the first to come back to me. I started the very next week."

"Why'd you drop out of uni?"

Sighing, I think back to how hard times were back then. "I couldn't afford to stay. It was kind of a pipe dream, really. I'm surprised I even managed the few months I did."

His eyes narrow as if he's trying to read more than the words I'm saying. I try to keep my expression neutral.

"What were you studying?"

"Business management and accounting."

"Do you regret it?"

I consider his question, because I'm not sure I have a simple answer. "Yes and no."

"Oh?"

"Yes because I'd have loved to be the first person in my family to graduate. I wanted to break the mould, smash anyone's preconceptions about my life and capabilities. It might have led me down a different path that would have hopefully meant less pain. No because...I'd never have met Lauren, Ben and the others and—"

"Me?" I can't help but laugh at the hopeful look on his face.

"Verdict's still out on that."

"Ouch." His hand comes up to cover his wounded heart. "I see how it is."

I fight the words that are on the tip of my tongue, but they tumble out, consequences be damned. "Things for me haven't always been easy. I need to know I'm surrounded by people I can trust, but gaining my trust isn't simple. I've been burned too many times by people who should care."

He nods and opens his mouth to say more, but the waiter arrives with our starters.

Thankfully, Trey changes the subject to lighter

topics. It's obvious that he just wants to learn more about me as he asks about my favourite films, music and food, but the little voice in the back of my mind still screams *why?* Why does a man like him want anything to do with a girl like me?

Dinner is incredible, just like the rest of today. I hate to think about how much this must be costing him. I still feel like a total fraud, being here surrounded by all these wealthy and put-together people while I feel like my world is once again on rocky ground.

Without wanting to, I've given Trey power.

He might not yet be able to shatter my heart into a million pieces, although I'm sure that won't be long, but if he were to turn around and tell me this was all one big joke then it would seriously hurt.

Worrying my bottom lip, I allow a large sigh to pass my lips, but it doesn't go unnoticed.

"What's wrong?"

"Nothing. This has been incredible, thank you so much."

"You don't look like you're enjoying yourself right now." His brows draw together and I chastise myself for being so transparent. I'm normally good at wearing a mask and hiding everything I'm feeling, but I have an inkling this man sees straight through that.

"No, I really am. I just can't help feeling like I don't fit." I look around at all the couples surrounding us. Most are at least ten years older than me. Trey fits in with his designer shirt and dominant demeanour, but me? Not so much.

"Everything I said earlier still stands. You're the most beautiful woman in this room. You belong here just as much as everyone else. Are you done?" He nods down to my empty coffee cup and I smile.

"Yeah." I'm so ready to have him all to myself and get what I've been waiting for all day.

"Fancy going for a walk?"

"Oh...uh...sure?"

With his hand on the small of my back, he guides me out of the hotel and into the brisk early winter evening.

"Here, it's cold." Shrugging off his jacket, he drapes it over my shoulders and pulls me to him.

Cuddled up against his side, I walk with him, enjoying the fresh air and his company, although it's not quite what I'd hoped we'd be doing by now.

We walk in a comfortable silence with the stars twinkling above us for the longest time. I almost miss the peacefulness of it when we eventually head back inside and up to our room.

"I just need to go and freshen up."

"Sure, take all the time you need."

Grabbing a few things from my suitcase, I lock myself in the bathroom and try to put all my doubts about this and him to the back of my mind. I want a night full of everything he can give me. Just two bodies and as much pleasure as we can manage before we pass out. I want our first night, the intensity that came with not knowing each other and the excitement of knowing it was only for a few hours.

Slipping out of my clothes, I pull my black lace nighty up my legs and rearrange my boobs so they look pert behind the fabric. I quickly reapply my red lipstick and fluff up my hair a little.

Once I'm happy, I pull the door open and wait for his eyes to find me.

I'm not disappointed. When they do, they widen and darken simultaneously.

"Fucking hell, Erica." My skin burns everywhere his eyes touch. All I can do is stand there and allow him to take his fill.

He's sitting on the edge of the bed in only his boxers, so I get to take in the view just as much as he does.

"Come here," he says, flipping the duvet over and patting the mattress. Disappointment floods me. Where is my dominant lover? Why's he not demanding that I get on my knees and suck him until he's dry?

Still, I follow his orders and climb onto the bed as sexily as I can. The second I'm lying down, he's beside me, wrapping his arm around my waist and pulling me back into him.

"Thank you for coming with me," he whispers in my ear as my blood starts to boil.

He just wants to fucking cuddle?

I lie still for a few seconds, hoping that this is a joke. He's acted like a perfect gentleman all day—aside from the incident on the massage table.

What the hell's going on?

This isn't the man I went home with that night or have been working beside the past couple of weeks. What. The. Hell?

When all he does is hold me tighter, I decide I need to take matters into my own hands if I'm going to end this day satisfied. His hard cock presses into my arse cheek so I know he's up for this.

Flipping over, I push my palm against his shoulder. His eyes widen in surprise but I swear his lips twitch up into a small smile. He allows me to move him, and the second I throw my leg over his waist, his hands land on my hips.

"What?" I snap when he looks up at me with amusement filling his eyes.

"Nothing. Have at it." His thumbs stroke across my hip and dip down to where my thighs meet. My core clenches, ready for what's about to come.

I grind down on him and his eyes flutter in pleasure. I knew he was just as on edge as I was.

Lifting up a little, I free him and take him in my hand. I lower myself onto his cock and we both moan as I sink down as far as I can go.

"Yesss," I hiss when he hits me so deep it borders on painful.

Placing my hands on his solid chest, I use him for leverage so I can lift almost all the way off before sinking straight back down.

The longer I look at him, the more I see the tension on his face. His lips press into a thin line, and the muscle in his neck pulses. He might be allowing me to take control right now, but he's not happy about it.

Tingles of my impending orgasm start to build almost immediately. I don't bother worrying if he's with me; selfishly, I focus solely on what I need. Hopefully it'll help pull him out of the nice act he's been putting on all day. Of course I want a nice guy beneath it all, but on the surface I need a little more rough around the edges. I need the arsehole I know is hiding within those steel eyes.

Grinding my hips, I ensure he hits me exactly

where I need it and, after only a few seconds, my pussy pulls him even deeper as my orgasm rocks my body. I throw my head back as I cry out his name, my hips slowing as I lose control of my muscles. Taking matters into his own hands, his fingers dig into my hips and he pistons in and out of me a few more times before his cock swells and his cum fills me.

Falling down onto him, both our chests heave as we try to catch our breaths.

"Fuck, yes," Trey says into the top of my head. If I weren't suddenly so exhausted I might tell him it's exactly what I've needed all day, too, but instead my eyes close and I fall fast asleep, still on top of him.

CHAPTER FOURTEEN

MY HEART DROPS when I reach out for him and all I find is an empty bed where he once slept. Propping myself up on my elbows, I cast my eyes around the room but he's not there. It's not until I register the sound of running water coming from the bathroom that my sleep-fogged brain realises where he is.

Slipping from the bed, I untwist my nighty from around my waist and head over, hoping that I'll find him in the waterfall shower.

Pushing the door open, I have to do a double-take at the sight before me. Trey is bent over a bath full of white fluffy bubbles, lighting candles that litter every surface of the room.

"What are you doing?"

"Oh, you're awake. I was coming to get you once I'd finished this."

"And what is this?"

"It's a bath...for you."

My frustration at how he's been acting suddenly gets the better of me. I don't mean to snap, but it's like I've lost control of my mouth. "Yeah, I can see that. But why? Why are you doing this, being all nice all of a sudden, treating me like I'm something special? What's the catch?"

"The catch?" His brows draw together as he looks between the bath and me, confused.

"Yeah. The catch. What do you want from me out of all this?"

"I don't want anything, Erica. I'm just being nice."

"That's bullshit. Every man wants something. It clearly isn't sex, because you were quite happy to go without last night. So what is it?"

"I just wanted to treat you, to make you happy."

"Not possible. I've never met a man who didn't have an ulterior motive, so come on, just admit it. You might as well confess now so I can decide if I want to continue with this charade any longer."

Trey's mouth opens like he has something he wants to say, but he closes it again, changing his mind. He takes a step toward me and I put my hands up to stop him. He pauses immediately, his eyes softening the longer he looks at me.

"Erica," he breathes, "I don't have an ulterior motive. I wanted to spend the weekend with you and get to know each other better. That really is it."

Tears burn the back of my throat and my eyes fill with water. "I don't believe you."

"Tough, because it's the truth." His voice is hard and it gives me a little hint of the man I thought I knew before this weekend. "I was trying to show you that not all men are arseholes. I was trying to be nice."

My emotions get the better of me and a sob bubbles up my throat. "Get out." My voice is barely above a whisper, but it doesn't need to be any louder. Trey gets the message loud and clear.

His shoulders drop, his eyes roaming over my face, trying to work me out, but thankfully he doesn't question me. He just nods once and walks past me, closing the door behind him.

Falling down on to the edge of the bath, I suck in a few lungfuls of air, hoping my random onslaught of tears subsides.

It's all Trey's fault.

He's playing with my emotions.

It's exactly why I didn't want to allow him to get too close in the first place. Now here I am, freaking out that he isn't what he says he is while desperately wanting to believe him. But trusting a man is dangerous. I've experienced that enough to know that I should never put my heart on the line. It's just not worth it.

I make the most of the bath because, despite what I said, it really was a nice thing to do. I need to thank him properly when I get out.

I take off yesterday's make-up and moisturise my entire body, anything to put off going out there and facing him after my meltdown. I'm stronger than to allow a man to affect me like this.

The room is empty when I cautiously step out. Thinking I've got a little reprieve from whatever he's going to say after showing him that side of me, I walk over to my case and drag out some clothes.

I've just pulled my t-shirt over my head when something out on the balcony catches my eye. Trey's sitting out there wearing a thick jumper and holding a steaming mugful of coffee in his hands, but that's not what really grabs my attention. It's the tableful of food in front of him. My stomach rumbles despite the three-course meal we consumed last night, and I put my concerns about seeing him to the back of my mind in favour of one of the pastries sitting in front of him.

His eyes fly to me the second I step out onto the

balcony. He must have heard me moving around in the room, but he allowed me the space I needed, something I'm very grateful for.

"How are you feeling?" Genuine concern fills his voice, and it makes me hate myself a little for accusing him of wanting something more than this from me.

"Better, thank you. This looks delicious."

"I wasn't sure what you'd want, so I asked for a selection of everything."

"It's really incredible." Reaching for a pastry, I waste no time in taking a bite and allowing the buttery goodness to melt on my tongue. I moan in pleasure and watch Trey's eyes darken.

"That good?" he asks, clearing his throat.

"Almost that good. Bite?"

"Sure."

I hold it up to his mouth and I'm fascinated as his full lips wrap around the sweet treat. My thighs clench, thinking back to those lips being on me only yesterday.

"Good, right?" I ask, trying to focus on the here and now.

He nods as he chews.

As we eat our way through about a week's worth of calories, I can see the million and one questions that fill his mind. I'm more grateful than I'd ever admit that he keeps them to himself.

The silence between us isn't awkward, but it's also not as comfortable as it has been in the past. I only have myself to blame.

"What did you want to do today?" he asks when the silence has stretched on a little too long.

"Well...um...I actually need to visit someone. It's something I do every Sunday morning, and she'll be expecting me, so I'm going to have to bail on any plans."

"I didn't have any plans. Can I take you?"

"Um..." The thought of showing him the side of my life that I try to keep buried has my heart racing, but the look of hope on his face stops me from denying him. I already feel bad enough about what happened in the bathroom, and I feel like I somehow need to make up for it.

"Sure. But then you can go and make the most of your day. I don't want to keep you longer than necessary."

His mouth opens to reply, but he must change his mind because in the end, all he does is nod.

It's no time at all before we're checking out and heading towards Trey's car. I hate that I've ruined our last few hours here, but there's not a lot I can do about it now. I've got a date to keep. Searching for the postcode on my phone, I plug it into Trey's Satnav and he's soon pulling out onto the main road and heading towards our destination.

"Who are you going to see?"

I hesitate, not sure if I want to open up about it or not, but seeing as he's going to see where we're headed in less than thirty minutes, I guess there's no point hiding it. "My mum. My sister and I usually do a yoga class together and then go and see her every Sunday."

"That's nice."

Is it? I wonder. Most Sundays are pure hell, but he's yet to understand the reality of the situation.

The second we turn in where the Satnav suggests, Trey's body tenses. I'm sure this place is far from what he was expecting.

The Park View Care Home signs are impossible to miss as we drive up toward the building. Trey looks over at me. From the corner of my eye, I can see his brows are drawn together in...concern or confusion, I'm not really sure.

"Just here's great. Thank you so much," I say when I spot Sam's car in her usual space. On a normal Sunday we'd arrive together, but not knowing what time I'd get here today, I told her to go on in without me. "It's been...really good."

I move to jump from the car, but the panic in his voice stops me. "Erica, wait."

I don't look back at him. I know that, if I do, everything I don't want to say to him will just fall from my mouth.

"I'll see you at work tomorrow. Thank you." With that, I slam his car door behind me and all but run towards the care home.

"Good morning, sweetie. We weren't sure if you were going to make it this morning," Sally, one of Mum's carers sings when I walk towards their desk.

I just about manage to bite back my short response about me being here *every* Sunday without fail. Poor Sally doesn't deserve to be on the wrong end of my mood right now. "Here I am. How is she?"

"Not good. She's sleeping now, was up most of the night apparently. Your sister's with her."

"Thank you."

I don't really even know why I feel so frustrated. After the luxury I've had for the past twenty-four hours, I really should be more relaxed than ever. I'm not sure if it's having to leave Trey or my residual anger from this morning, but the closer I get to Mum's room, the tighter my muscles get.

My steps slow as I approach her open door, just like they do every time. I hate being here. I hate seeing her like this. But I still do it every Sunday without fail like it's expected of me. And I guess in some ways, it is. But if I were to think back to all her failings as a mother, I'm sure no one could criticize if I were to turn my back.

"Hey," I whisper as I round the corner, knowing exactly what seat I'll find my sister sitting in.

The moment she registers it's me, she jumps to the edge of her seat, a smile playing on her lips. "How was it?"

Blowing out a breath, I walk over and gently kiss Mum's forehead before falling down onto my seat and looking toward my overly excited sister.

"It was...over the top, expensive, incredible, scary."

"Scary?"

"I'm just trying to figure out what his angle is, what he wants."

"Does he have to want anything more than you?"

"Always. Men always want more."

"There will be one who doesn't, Erica. You need to give it enough time to figure out if he's that one." She stares at me for a few seconds as her words settle in my head. "Anyway, he is seriously hot for an older man."

A genuine laugh falls from my lips and I immediately feel lighter. Sam has a way of making everything seem that little bit more bearable.

Mum stays asleep the whole time we visit. As usual when this is the case, we leave a little note and a couple of very questionable drawings for her to look at when she's able. It's horrible, sitting there knowing she has no idea we've visited, especially as we're both very aware that no one else will be here until this time next Sunday, but what else can we do? It's not like we can put our lives on hold for however long she's going to be here. Plus, the chances of her knowing who we are or being aware that we're in the room even if she was awake are slim.

We're chatting away as we walk out through the care home entrance when I suddenly stop.

"What's wrong?"

"He's still here." I've no idea why I whisper; it's not like he could hear me from inside his car at the other side of the car park, anyway.

"Did you tell him to go?"

"Uh..." I think back over our awkward conversation before I ran from his car. "Well, no, but I thought I made it quite clear not to stay."

He must feel my stare, because his eyes lift and find mine. A smile curls his lips while my heart starts to race.

"I think you've found yourself a keeper there."

Her words barely register. The only thing I can really hear is my blood whooshing past my ears.

"I don't...I'm not..."

"Pull yourself together, woman," my sister laughs.

We both watch, Sam excited, me in total disbelief, as Trey pushes the car door open so he can greet me.

"Well? What are you waiting for? Go to him. Go and thank him properly for sitting out here all this time."

"I don't know."

"Erica, you've got to trust someone one day."

With those few words ringing in my ears, I make my way towards him. His smile only gets wider the closer I get. Regret twists my stomach for how I treated him this morning. Maybe my sister's right. Maybe I do need to try to trust him.

"Hey, you didn't have to wait."

"I know. I wanted to." His hand finds mine and his fingers squeeze. My heart damn near explodes. No one's ever actually wanted to do something like that for me before. "What? You're looking at me like my skin's suddenly turned purple or something."

"You really sat out here waiting this whole time?"

"I did."

"I'm sorry about this morning. I acted like—"

"It's okay." His spare hand comes up to tuck a lock of hair behind my ear, and his thumb brushes my cheek. It's so gentle that it makes my chin tremble.

"You fancy going for coffee?"

"That sounds perfect."

As I turn back to walk around to the car, I find my sister where I left her, grinning like an idiot.

CHAPTER FIFTEEN

THE REMAINDER of the day passes all too fast, and before I know it we're back in Trey's car to head home.

I rest my head back and take a few deep breaths.

"Are you okay?"

"Yeah, I really am. Thank you for today."

"You're more than welcome."

He took me for coffee as he suggested and then we ended up walking around a park I'd never been to before. On the way back, we passed a cute Italian restaurant and Trey insisted on taking me for dinner.

The day was totally unexpected but exactly what I needed. I'd managed to lose the idea that it was any more than two people enjoying each other's company thanks to my sister's words of advice, and I couldn't be more grateful.

"Oh shit," I gasp. At some point, I'd managed to shut my eyes, and now we're a street away from my sister's place.

"What's wrong?"

"Um…" I stall, wondering if I really want to trust him. In the end, it's not really a hard decision to make. "I don't actually live here."

"Okay. So where do you live?" He glances over at me, his eyes wide as he waits for an answer.

"Please don't hate me."

"Why? Where do you live, Erica?"

"Just drive to your place."

"My place?"

His eyes leave the road briefly and he looks at me, his brow creased with confusion, but he puts the indicator on and does as I suggest.

"You live on the same street?"

"Something like that."

"So whose house did I pick you up from yesterday?"

"My sister's."

"Why?"

"Because I was scared."

"Of?"

"You, me…this."

"You're going to need to spell it out for me a little more here, Erica."

"Just go and park, and I'll explain."

In minutes he's pulling into his allocated parking spot outside our building. He cuts the engine and turns to me.

"Go on."

"That first night. It was meant to just be a one-night thing. I didn't want to tell the truth when I discovered where you lived in case you wanted a repeat, or worse—"

"Worse?"

"I'm a mess, Trey. I've been screwed over by more men than I care to admit, and I had—have—no intention of history repeating itself. So one-nighters were all I had to offer. I promised myself that I was keeping my heart out of everything to do with men. No feelings, no attachments, and no repeats. Then I met you and you brought me here. I didn't think it would matter. I'd never see you again, and really the chances of meeting in the stairwell were pretty slim."

"Wait... you live in this building?"

"I do. I actually live below you."

"Below me?" His eyes widen as he processes what I just said. "All this time you've been right here and I had no idea?" I nod, biting down on my bottom lip, concerned about how he's going to take this. "So the night you left me that voicemail, you were mere feet away. The next morning when you ran into me on the stairs, you weren't there because you'd come to see me? Jesus." He scrubs his hand over his face and I panic that I've just ruined everything.

"I was—I am—scared, Trey. I was worried that—"

"It's okay." Reaching over, he takes my cheek in his hand, his thumb pulling my bottom lip from being attacked by my teeth. "I understand. Frustrated as hell that I couldn't come down and take what I needed whenever I wanted, but I get it."

"Really?"

He doesn't answer. Instead, he leans over the centre console and brushes his lips against mine. My entire body relaxes the second we connect. It should scare me but really, it just feels right.

He pulls back all too soon. I'm tempted to wrap my fist in his shirt and pull him back to me until I spot someone out of the corner of my eye and realise we've got an audience.

"Come up, let's get you up to your flat."

With our bags in hand, we make our way up to my floor. I expect him to invite himself in but, to my surprise, after he's dropped my case inside the door he steps back. "So you really live beneath me?"

"I really do. I'm sorry I didn't tell you." The guilt of lying to him, even though I know he understands, still eats at me.

We're locked in our stare when a deep, rumbling

voice comes from behind me. "Glad you brought her back in one piece."

"I also should probably have warned you that that idiot is my flatmate."

"Hey," he argues, "you know your life's been better since I moved in. Don't even try to deny it."

"Was it only me who didn't know?" Now Trey looks pissed off. His eyes have hardened and his lips press into a thin line.

"Know what?" Joe asks innocently.

"That I live upstairs."

"You live upstairs?" Joe goes to the effort of pointing above his head just in case the words aren't enough. "Oh my god." Shaking my head at Joe, I try to stop what I know is about to come. "The night you pulled him, I spent the night down here getting myself off to the hot sex going on upstairs. *That was you!*"

I'm not usually one to get embarrassed by my shenanigans, but this has just hit my limit. Stepping forward, I drop my forehead to Trey's shoulder. It vibrates with his laughter and I groan.

"Yeah, man. That night was pretty hot. If I knew she was this close it might have happened a few more times since, too."

"I'm so looking forward to the coming weeks."

"And I'm looking forward to you moving out," I say as seriously as possible, turning to look at him.

"Aw, don't be like that, sweets. You love having me here and you know it."

"Uh huh."

"I'm going to leave you two to argue this out." Trey grabs my hand and pulls me into his chest. His lips drop to my ear and my skin tingles. "I'll see you tomorrow. Fancy a lift to work?"

"That would be awesome, thank you."

"My pleasure. You know where I am if you need me."

"You too."

He leaves me with a toe-curling kiss, making me want to drag him to my bedroom and let him do all kinds of other wicked things to my body. Instead, I allow him to back away and close the door when he hits the stairs.

"He lives up-fucking-stairs. Were you ever going to tell me?" I shrug because telling Joe about it was the least of my worries. "Well, if it helps at all, from listening to the two of you I'd suggest you go up there more often. Hell, move in with him if it means you get that kind of action regularly."

"You're a fucking nightmare. I'm going to unpack."

"You want dinner?"

"No, I ate with Trey."

"Ooh, this really is getting serious."

I don't respond, mainly because I don't have an answer. I'm terrified of it being true and having my heart trampled on once again, but at the same time I also can't stop myself from starting to fall.

IF I THOUGHT it was frustrating before listening to him move around upstairs, then it's downright torturous now. Every creak of the floorboards above and my body's on full alert.

"Just go up there already," Joe suggests from the other end of the sofa where we're sitting watching the TV.

"I'm good."

"No, you're not. You're coiled like a bloody spring. Go and surprise him and let him fuck your brains out."

"I'm trying not to get attached," I whisper, not really wanting to admit it out loud.

"How's that working out for you?"

I stay where I am for a few seconds, feeling a little sorry for myself before jumping up.

"That's my girl," Joe calls from behind me.

"I'm going to the kitchen for hot chocolate. Don't

get excited, I don't intend on being your personal porn star tonight."

"Shame. I could do with some."

"You never came home Friday night. I'm assuming you hooked up?" I call, hoping for some details on his sex life to get the heat off me.

"Yes, I met this couple who wanted to, uh...spice things up."

"You spent the night with a couple?"

"Sure did, sweets."

"Were you for her or him?"

"Both."

"No way," I say with a laugh. I know Joe's a bit of a player, but that's a bit much, even for him.

"Deadly serious. It was pretty incredible."

"I'll take your word for it!"

"You're seriously planning on spending the night with me and a mug of hot chocolate that doesn't even have marshmallows on?"

"If you keep going on, I'll be spending the evening in my room with my mug of marshmallow-less hot chocolate."

Joe eventually stops giving me grief and we spend the evening enjoying the slightly boring Sunday night TV and putting the world to rights.

When I walk into my room ready to get into bed, my phone lights up on the bedside table. Seeing

Trey's name, I immediately swipe the screen and open the message.

> Trey: Thank you for an incredible weekend. Sleep tight x

Butterflies erupt in my belly, knowing that he's right above my head, thinking about me. Feeling cheeky, I send my own message back.

> Erica: How's it feel, knowing I'm beneath you yet you can't touch?

I wait for a few seconds, but when his response doesn't come I force myself to go into the bathroom.

Too anxious to find out if he's replied, I rush back to my bed the second I flush the toilet to see if it's there. I squeal in delight when I see his name. My heart thunders in my chest so much that I can feel it in my toes.

> Trey: Get up here now.

There's my demanding, dominant Trey, I think as I pull out my bottom drawer to find something suitable for my visit.

"Fucking knew you'd cave," Joe calls out when he spots me running towards the front door.

"Turn the music up, yeah?"

"I will do no such fucking thing. Make sure you're loud," is the last thing I hear before the door slams behind me.

I probably should cover up to make the short journey up the stairs, but it's too late now. With my head held high, I make my way to his door.

Knocking, I lean against the doorframe and plaster what I hope is a seductive look on my face.

It takes a few seconds but, before long, the sound of his footsteps hits my ears. My stomach knots as anticipation for his reaction hits me full force.

"I didn't think you'd ever get...Get the fuck in here." His fingers wrap around my wrist and I'm harshly pulled inside his flat. I stumble on my heels but he keeps me upright before the door's slammed and I'm pushed back against it.

His eyes are dark and wide, his nostrils flare and his lips part, his increased breath tickling my face.

"Don't fucking ever walk up here looking like that again. You hear me?"

"Yes, Sir," I whisper, looking up at him through my lashes, and it only spurs him on. His eyes get impossibly dark, the muscle in his neck pulsating with need.

He takes a step back from me and I panic until his eyes drop to my black satin covered body. The baby doll has a split all the way up the front and is held together with a red bow under my boobs. The G-string that barely covers me is the same fire engine red, and so are my shoes. My skin burns as his eyes trail over me, my core clenching with need for the release I hope he's going to give me.

"You're going to fucking pay for that. No one, other than me, ever gets the chance to see you dressed like this. Understand?"

"Yes."

"Now...what the fuck shall I do to you?"

"Anything," I breathe.

Reaching back, he pulls his t-shirt over his head and drops it to the floor before undoing the tie around his jogging bottoms. He walks over to the sofa, drops them and falls down on the edge, legs spread wide, his hard cock begging for my attention.

"What the fuck are you waiting for? Get over here and suck me."

My body moves before my brain even realises, and I'm lowering myself to my knees in front of him.

I wrap my hand around his length as his fingers find their way into my hair so he can pull me forward and take what he needs.

"Fuck," he barks when he hits the back of my throat. His hips lift from the sofa with his need for more.

Pulling back, I lick around the head of his cock

before sinking back down. His length twitches and he growls.

"Not. In. Your. Mouth." His fingers grip painfully in my hair and I'm pulled off of him.

Kicking his joggers off, he stands and lifts me with his hands on my arse. His lips drop to mine and his tongue sweeps into my mouth. I hungrily accept what he gives, tangling my own tongue with his and sucking on it harshly, his moan of pleasure vibrating up his chest.

He starts walking and I expect us to end up in his bedroom, but about halfway there my back is pressed up against the cold wall. His hips pin me in place as he rips the tiny bit of red fabric from around my waist.

"Can't wait," he grunts, lining himself up with my entrance and dropping me onto his cock.

I cry out at the sudden invasion, not giving two shits about our eavesdropper downstairs.

"Fuck, Trey. Fuck."

"So fucking wet."

My walls clamp down around him as he simultaneously thrusts and lowers me to ensure he hits me as deep as possible.

"Fuck, fuck, fuck," I chant as my release gets ever closer. This is what I needed all weekend. Yes, I want a nice guy, I want him to treat me right, do all the sweet things he's done over the past few days, but when we close the door at night, this is exactly what I need. I need demands, and orders, and this sexy dominant lover who's guaranteed to make me scream time after fucking time.

"Trey," I cry, my body tensing and convulsing as my orgasm flows though me.

He continues with his punishing pace as my pleasure starts to fade. He swells within me, his fingers digging tighter into my arse as he approaches the end.

His head drops back and he roars like a wild fucking animal as he fills me.

The moment he can move, he's carrying me down to his bedroom and throwing me down on the bed. I drop my eyes to get a sight of his arse as he walks towards his dresser.

"Tonight, you're mine. You do what I say when I say it. Got it?"

"Got it." There's absolutely no hesitation in my voice, and, when he turns to look at me, I swear I see pride shining in his dark eyes.

Bring it fucking on, big man.

CHAPTER SIXTEEN

"YOU READY?" Joe calls through my bedroom door.

"Give me a second." I'm ready—I have been for about ten minutes, but I think I spun around too fast because I've gone all light-headed.

I suck in a few more deep breaths, hoping it'll ease it. Ben announced an impromptu night out this afternoon after he signed off on the job Joe had been running. It was a huge warehouse renovation and we were pretty much relying on it paying off to clear a huge chunk of the company's debt. It's been a stressful few weeks as we've waited for something to go wrong or for someone to demand repayment earlier than they'd agreed.

Pushing myself from the bed, I slip my feet into my trainers and join him.

"Are you okay?" *I'm glad I look as good as I feel,* I think as I head toward the front door.

"Yeah, I'm good. Just relieved things are starting to look up."

"I told you it was all going to be fine."

"I know. I just still feel so guilty that this whole disaster wouldn't have happened if it weren't for me and my bad decision making."

"Stop beating yourself up. He manipulated you into doing his dirty work, just like the rest of us."

"How are things with Lauren?" He hasn't been spending nearly as much time with her as he would have in the past, and I know he misses her more than he'll ever admit.

"They're okay. I hate that I can see doubt in her eyes every time she looks at me. It's like she's trying to work out what else I'm lying about. That was the only time I've ever deceived her. I know it doesn't really matter now, but I was just trying to protect her."

"I know. She'll come around. Just give her time. We hurt her pretty badly."

The sound of Trey's hard knock sounds out around the flat.

We're both silent as Joe pulls the door open, and I'm soon distracted when Trey's revealed, wearing a skin-tight polo shirt and a slim pair of jeans.

"Wow," I breathe.

"I was thinking the same." His eyes drop from mine to take in my body. I don't really think the jeans and t-shirt I'm wearing are worthy of that kind of attention, but I won't argue. My body heats up under his scrutiny, making me wish we weren't about to spend the night bowling with our colleagues.

"Let's go before you two start fucking in the hallway."

Trey opens his mouth to respond but, like me, he must decide it's pointless and instead grabs my hand and pulls me from the flat, allowing Joe to lock up.

"Well, this is a little more fancy than I'm used to," Joe says, bouncing up and down on the back seat of Trey's Jaguar like a little kid, making Trey wince.

"Yeah, and I'd appreciate it if you didn't break it."

Laughing at the two of them, I buckle myself in and sit back. My head's still feeling a little weird, but I'm hopeful some fast food will sort me right out.

We all meet for burgers before heading towards the bowling alley. I've no idea why Ben decided on this. I haven't been since I was a kid, and that was only for friends' birthday parties. Sadly, this kind of thing wasn't an everyday occurrence for my family.

Ben and Lauren bicker as they put everyone's names into the little computer ready for our game to start, while Joe finds all the heavy balls to show off with. Rolling my eyes at him, I allow Trey to pull me down onto the bench beside him.

"I can't remember the last time I did this."

"Me either. It should be fun."

"You don't look like you mean that."

Plastering a smile on my face, I look up at him. His brows are drawn together in concern as his eyes flit all over me, trying to find what might be wrong. "I do. I think I've just eaten too much," I say as my stomach turns over once again. The burger and chips might have been a little too much after only eating a few biscuits all day.

"Okay," he says, although he doesn't look like he means it. "If you need to leave, just say."

"I'm good, I promise."

I manage to do my first couple of throws fine, although I totally miss each time—unlike Trey who, after only the first round, was already topping the leader board. It seems he might have a hidden talent for bowling.

My body temperature suddenly spikes and my mouth waters like I'm going to throw up. I suck in a deep breath and fan my hand in front of me.

"I'm taking you home."

"No, no. I'm having fun." My argument is weak at best. The only thing I want to do right now is curl up in my bed but I don't want to let anyone down.

"It wasn't a question."

Trey stands and says something to Ben and Lauren who both turn to me, concern written all over their faces. They smile, but they're nowhere near genuine. I can only imagine how bad I must be looking.

I'm pulled up against Trey's side and, after saying quick goodbyes to everyone, we change back into our shoes and head out towards his car.

"I'm so sorry," I whisper once he's backing out of the space.

"Don't be silly. You're ill. Everyone can see that."

"Brilliant," I mutter, a humourless laugh falling from my lips.

"That's not what I meant, and you know it. You look as beautiful as ever."

I scoff at his comment but don't respond. Instead, I rest my head back and will my stomach to settle.

"What are you doing?" I ask when Trey pulls the car to a stop out the front of a row of shops.

"Do you need anything?"

"Sleep."

"Okay, wait here."

I don't get a chance to demand that he stays put and just drives me home, because he's out of the car and marching towards the shop doors before I have a chance to think.

He's not gone all that long. I watch his every movement as his long, denim-clad legs carry him back towards me. I run my eyes up the fitted t-shirt that shows off his sculpted muscles beneath and, despite feeling like shit, tingles erupt between my legs at just the sight alone.

"Here," he says, dropping into the driver's seat and passing me a bag.

"What's this?"

"A few things to make you feel better."

Opening the bag, I stare down at the contents. Instantly, my eyes fill with tears and emotion burns my throat.

"You—" I don't manage to get any more words out, the giant lump clogging my throat stopping me.

"I what?" Trey starts the engine before turning to look at me. "Shit, what's wrong?"

Fighting against the emotions warring inside me, I swallow and force out some words. "You bought all this for me?" My voice is barely above a whisper, and it gives away everything I'm feeling.

"Yeah, I wanted to do something to make you feel better. Is that...okay?" He hesitates as my first tears fall. Dragging my eyes from his, I look back down into the bag. There's some medicine to settle my stomach and some painkillers, but it's the giant bar of chocolate, tub of ice cream, bottle of bubble bath and candles that do me in.

A sob rumbles up my throat and I'm powerless to stop the tears that follow.

"Fuck, I was only trying to do something nice. I can take it all back?"

"No, no," I manage through my sobs. "These are happy tears."

"Really?"

"Really. This is just...it's everything."

"It's just a few things from the corner shop. I didn't exactly go to a lot of effort."

"Effort doesn't matter, Trey. It's the thought behind it. That's...well, it's more than I've ever had."

His face hardens and I kick myself for once again revealing a part of my past I'd rather no one knows about.

"Erica," he breathes, reaching over and taking my hand in one of his and wiping my tears away with the other. "You deserve so much more than what you've had in the past. Let me in, let me show you how it should be."

My tears almost immediately dry at his words, at his demand for me to drop the walls I've spent so many years painstakingly constructing.

Shaking my head, I watch as his features darken with disappointment. "I can't," I whisper, ripping my eyes from his and staring at the dark night surrounding us.

My stomach turns over, but this time it's not with whatever bug I've picked up, it's with the regret that floods me the second those two words leave my lips.

Trey deserves more than me. He deserves someone who can allow him into her life, to show him exactly who she is. Tears burn again, but this time I fight like hell to stop them from dropping.

I don't register any of the trip home. The next thing I know, Trey's warm palm lands on my thigh, and when I look up I find that we're parked in front of our building.

"How are you feeling?"

Numb. "A little better, thank you."

The genuine concern on his face has my heart aching. I so badly want this thing between us to be something. I've refused to allow myself to fantasize about it for fear of it not happening, but little thoughts about him being the one for me keep creeping their way in.

"Come on, let's get you inside."

He has my door open and my hand in his before I get a chance to think about it. He leads me up to my flat and takes the keys from my hand once I've dug them out of my bag.

He doesn't once let go of my other hand, and the

second we're inside with the door shut he pulls me up against his chest.

His thumb brushes my cheek and he tucks a lock of my hair behind my ear. "What do you need?"

Well, if that isn't a loaded question. I have a million answers on the tip of my tongue.

I swallow them all down and squeak out a safe one. "A bath."

"You go and get sorted and I'll run it for you."

I stop when I get to my room and watch as he continues down the hall to the main bathroom.

Chewing on my bottom lip, I wonder what it would be like to let him in. To tell him all my dark secrets that I keep locked away from everyone.

He must feel my stare because when he gets to the door, he stops and looks over his shoulder. The intensity in his eyes makes my breath catch. Where I'm doing my best to hide what he does to me, how he feels is written all over his face.

Maybe trusting him wouldn't be so bad.

"THAT WAS QUICK," Trey says, poking his head around my bedroom door after I've finished my bath.

"I got a little hot," I lie. In reality, I just hated being in there alone while he was sitting on my sofa, but I daren't tell him that I missed him. That's crazy.

"Feeling any better?"

"I am, actually. I might give that ice cream a try."

"You must be feeling better," he says with a laugh as I follow him out to the living room. "Sit down. I'll get it for you."

Relaxing on the sofa while he crashes around in the kitchen feels surreal. Since the day Sam and I moved out of our family home, I've only ever looked after myself.

"I'm assuming you want the tub?"

"How else would I eat it?"

"Here." He passes the tub and a spoon to me as he falls down beside me with his own.

"Uh...what are you doing?" I ask when he moves to take some ice cream.

"I was going to have some. Am I not allowed?"

"How much do you know about women?"

"Not enough, apparently. So...I can't have any?"

"Just because you were really sweet and got it for me, I'll allow it. But," I say in a rush, "not too much."

A wide smile spreads across his face as he digs in.

"Whoa, whoa, I said not too much." My eyes almost pop out of my head when I take in the giant lump of ice cream on his spoon.

"This is it. The rest is yours."

The second his lips wrap around the spoon, I forget all about sharing ice cream. He knows I'm watching and makes a show of licking the spoon clean and ensuring his moan of pleasure is loud enough to hit exactly where he intends. My thighs clench and suddenly the only thing I'm interested in having in my mouth is him.

"So your sister's getting married." I get whiplash at his sudden change of topic. My brows draw together in confusion until he helps me out. "The invite is on the front of your fridge."

"Oh right, yeah. It feels like she's been planning it forever. I can't believe it's almost here." I shovel a spoonful of ice cream into my mouth, my eyes flutter shut and a moan rumbles up my throat as the sweet creaminess melts on my tongue.

Trey shifts in his seat beside me and I look over, a smug smile on my lips.

"What about your family?" Somehow I've revealed much more than I intended to with his visit to the care home car park and knowing a little about my sister.

"Um..." he mumbles as he continues his attempt to get comfortable, "my parents both retired and moved out to the Cotswolds a few years ago, and my older brother is an investment banker, total workaholic."

"Is he married?"

"He has been," he says with a chuckle. "She was just after his money. It didn't last long."

The conversation flows easily between us as we both reveal little bits of our lives. Trey seems totally relaxed as he tells me about his childhood and his career, whereas my muscles lock up tight every time he asks me a question.

"What about your dad?"

"He's gone. Walked out years ago." I don't intend on explaining any more, but when he turns his eyes on me the words just keep flowing. "He wasn't a nice man. He controlled every aspect of our lives and kept Mum in line with his harsh, belittling words. Life at home was never great, but when I was nine, it all went downhill.

"I came home from a friend's house earlier than planned and walked in on Dad with another woman. Everything got a whole lot worse after that. He blackmailed me, told me no one would ever believe a child, that they would all think I was a liar because he loved my mother—that's what the outside world thought, anyway. He never physically hurt any of us that I'm aware of, although if he stuck around any longer I'm sure it would have happened. He was a monster, and only the beginning of a long line of them." I regret the final words the second they slip out, but it's too late now. Although he's never said anything about the reason behind the business' failings and how I played a part in it, I'm under no illusion he must know what went on between Nick and me. "I told myself I'd never be that weak again. After being used and abused more times than I can count, I told myself I'd give up on men. And then..."

"Here I am."

"Here you are." I put the empty ice cream tub and spoon down on the coffee table and Trey takes my hand, stopping me from getting up and instead turning me towards him.

I keep my eyes down, too afraid of what he'll see in them after my little trip down memory lane.

"Look at me," he demands, and just like the little girl who followed all her daddy's orders, I look up, immediately finding his eyes.

"I'm not like them." His palm cups my cheek as he stares deep into my eyes, willing me to believe him.

"Everyone wants something," I whisper, hating that I sound so vulnerable.

"I do want something, Erica." My breath catches at his admission. "I want you."

CHAPTER SEVENTEEN

WHEN I WAKE the next morning it's with Trey's arm laying heavily across my waist and his breath tickling down my neck.

"Morning." His deep, rough voice has tingles erupting in all the right places. I grind my arse back into him and he groans. "As much as I'd love that, I've got an early meeting to get to."

"You should have woken me earlier."

"You're ill. I wanted you to sleep."

I pout as I continue to rub up against him. He soon reacts. I'm flipped onto my back and my bottom lip is sucked into his mouth.

"Ow," I complain when he bites down.

"Punishment for teasing me," he says with a cheeky smile and a wink when he pulls back. "I really need to go."

Standing, I watch as he stretches and turns towards me. My eyes run over his exposed skin and down to the very obvious tent in his boxers.

"I could be real quick."

"I don't want to enjoy you quickly, Erica. I want to savour ever minute." Lust shoots through me but he stands by his words and turns towards his discarded clothes.

I sit myself up against the headboard with the intention of watching his muscles ripple beneath his skin as he dresses, but the moment I move, my stomach turns over.

Holding my breath, I will it to disappear before he turns and notices.

"I'll make it up to you tonight," he promises as he turns back toward me. "On second thoughts, maybe you should call in sick."

"I can't, I've got too much to do."

"You're better off here if you're ill."

I shrug off his concerns and, after a chaste kiss, I send him on his way. It's only once he's gone that I appreciate how terrible I feel. I probably should call in, but I still feel like I've got so much to prove, so instead I shove to my feet and push through the sick feeling turning in my stomach.

"YOU MISSED A FUCKING AWESOME NIGHT, E. You should have—fuck."

I've no idea what comes over me, but the second Ben turns to look at me, I burst into tears. "What's wrong?" He walks over, throws his arms around me and pulls me against him. It only makes me cry harder, but I've no idea why. I'm not a crier. I've perfected the art of putting on a brave face and battling my way through.

This. Is. Not. Me.

He doesn't let up until I've got my breathing under control, but even then he hardly releases his hold as he pulls back to look at me. "What's wrong? Has Trey done something?" Anger twitches at the sides of his lips and the muscle in his neck pulses.

"What? No, no, Trey's not done anything. He's good, really good, actually."

"So what's wrong? The last woman I knew who burst into tears like that was pre—" The look of pure horror on my face is enough to cut off that final word, but I hear it loud and clear. His arms release me and I stumble backwards, my chest heaving.

"Fuck."

"Erica?"

My trembling hand comes up to cover my mouth as I think back over the previous few days. The sick feeling, the light-headedness. *When was my last period exactly?* I rack my brain but come up empty.

"No, no. I can't be. I'm on the pill. It's just a bug."

"Stranger things have happened."

"Fuck." Resting my palms on the counter, I drag in a few deep breaths. *This cannot be happening.*

"Why don't you take the day off? Go figure out what's going on. Get some rest, you look exhausted. I'm sure Lauren would come if you want some company."

"No, it's fine. I think I need to do this alone."

"That's what I was afraid of." Glancing over my shoulder at his concerned face, my heart drops. I hate being a disappointment. "Please don't shut us out, Erica. We're here to help you."

"I know, and I promise I won't. This is just something that I need to get my head around myself first, if it even is a thing." Even as I say the words, I know I'm only lying to myself. How I didn't suspect anything before now is beyond me. All the signs have been there. If I'd just pulled my head out of my arse and used my brain instead of pining after Trey like a love-sick teenager, I might have seen this coming.

"Call us if you need anything," Ben shouts as I get to the door.

Looking back over my shoulder, I manage a weak smile before turning back the way I came only minutes ago. I grab my bag from where I dropped it on my desk and walk straight out.

Lauren's walking around the side of the house as I leave, but I don't acknowledge her. I don't need to. Ben will tell her everything in about thirty seconds, I'm sure.

I should probably call a taxi—it will get me where I need to be faster—but at no point do I reach into my bag for my phone. Instead, I just keep walking. I walk, feeling totally numb and utterly stupid for being so blindsided by this. I'm an intelligent woman. It should not have taken my male best friend to point this out to me.

By the time I stumble across a chemist, I've convinced myself that this is all one big joke. So what, I'm a little emotional? It doesn't have to mean anything.

I can't look at the cashier as she scans the test and asks me if I want a bag. I decline the offer and shove the box straight into my handbag—out of sight, out of mind. I throw some cash at her and get the hell out before anyone sees me.

I intend on going home to do it in private, but when I spot a Starbucks before I get to the tube station I find myself walking inside and straight towards the toilets.

The last place I want to do this is in a public

bathroom, but now the test is in my possession, my need to find out is too strong.

I lock myself in the last cubicle and pull the box from my bag. I read the instructions, trying to register what the words are telling me, but other than the final result everything passes me by. I know the gist of these things; I've heard them spoken about enough. Pee on the stick and wait for your fate to be decided. So that's what I do.

I balance the little bit of plastic upside down on the toilet roll holder as I right my clothing and begin pacing the tiny space.

I'm not. I can't be. Ben's wrong. I'm just putting too much on myself with work and I'm exhausted. No matter how many times I repeat those words in my head, I know they're not true.

Glancing down at my phone, it confirms that enough time has passed. I take a long, slow breath and shake my hands out, hoping they'll stop trembling, and reach out for the test.

Squeezing my eyes shut, I turn it over, count to three and then look.

Pregnant. "Fuck." I stumble back and crash into the cubicle wall.

"Are you okay?" someone calls out.

"Y-yeah, thanks." I've no idea if it comes out loud

enough for anyone to hear; I'm too focused on that one little word.

That one little word that has the power to change my life.

I've no idea how I managed it, but somehow I find my way out of Starbucks and onto a tube heading toward home. Everything around me is a blur; all I can see is that one word.

When I eventually make it home, I drop my bag in the hallway, kick off my shoes and curl up on my bed.

I don't cry, I don't scream. I don't do anything. I'm just numb.

I MANAGE to drag my pathetic arse out of bed, ready for Joe to come home. I try to make myself look a little presentable, but when I glance in the mirror in the hallway I realise I've failed miserably.

I kick-start the coffee machine so I can have a mug ready for him. I've noticed over the past couple of weeks that he's started going out on Thursday nights, although I don't think it's the kind of night out he's used to as he's usually home before ten.

He appears right on time and, as he walks towards me, I push his steaming mug of black coffee towards him, trying to ignore the churning of my stomach as the scent fills my nose.

"Are you okay? Ben said he sent you home."

"I'll be fine. You out tonight?"

Something passes across his face but it's gone too quickly for me to be able to read. "Uh…yeah?"

"This is turning into a regular thing. Have you met someone?" I ask, disappointed that he hasn't even mentioned it if he has.

"What? No," he says, a little too defensively. "I've just been meeting a friend." I don't believe a word of it, and the fact that he can't hold my eyes as he says it confirms that he's not telling me the whole story. "Thanks for the coffee. I need to shower." He turns back before he leaves the room and drops a kiss to my cheek. "Thank you," he whispers before disappearing. I've no idea what he's thanking me for. Shrugging at his elusiveness, I take my glass of water over to the sofa to find something to stare at on the TV.

Joe reappears dressed to impress, including his thick-rimmed glasses that make him look like a sexy bad boy nerd, and rushes out of the door. It makes me even more suspicious about what he's up to.

Resting back, my stomach rumbles. I don't really want to eat anything, knowing it'll probably only make me feel sick, but guilt tugs at my insides. I need to start looking after myself.

I just get to the kitchen when there's a knock on the door. Peeking through the peephole, my heart begins to race as I find Trey on the other side. Ben wouldn't have said anything, would he?

I take a couple of deep breaths, hold my head high and pull the door open.

"Hey, are you feeling any better? Ben said you were pretty rough this morning. Did you get worse after I left?"

"Yeah, eating something before leaving the house didn't really help."

"Are you hungry now? I brought soup."

My stomach growls loudly right on cue, distracting Trey from the tears once again filling my eyes at his thoughtfulness.

"Yes, come on in. I'll get bowls."

It turns out that Trey not only bought soup but also a freshly baked loaf of bread and a new tub of ice cream after I polished off the one he got me last night with gusto. Something about the cold sweetness really helped to settle my stomach, and tonight is the same.

"You've got a little colour back in your cheeks. Chicken soup really does fix everything."

I mumble my agreement but, in reality, soup is never going to fix what I'm hiding right now.

I should tell him, I know that, but the idea of allowing the actual words past my lips has the beginnings of a panic attack clawing at my lungs. I need to figure out how I feel about this before I even think about getting Trey's perspective. Our relationship might have been becoming more serious lately, but we're still quite a way from the marriage and kids talk. I'm worried this new development is going to ruin everything we're been building together.

"If you're feeling better tomorrow, will you have dinner with me? I want to take you to my favourite restaurant."

"That sounds good. I told Ben I'd stay off tomorrow as well, so it'll be nice to get out of the house."

He nods, pulls me into his side and kisses the top of my head. I allow myself to relax into his warmth and fight to keep thoughts of our future out of my mind.

I end up falling asleep beside him. I'm vaguely aware of him carrying me to bed and sliding in beside me, but that's it. The next time I wake, I'm once again alone in my bed with only thoughts of my reality to keep me company.

CHAPTER EIGHTEEN

AFTER ANOTHER DAY lying on the sofa watching reruns of *Friends* for the millionth time, I'm glad I agreed to go out tonight. I've grazed on beige food all day, and eating little and often has helped keep my sickness at bay.

As much as I've tried to tell myself that I can keep this a secret, I know I'm only lying to myself. Trey deserves to know about what's really wrong with me. After all, it takes two to tango, and although I reassured him that I was on the pill, we're both intelligent adults who know that it's not one hundred percent effective. There's always a risk. The chance might be low but unfortunately we're now some of the unlucky—or lucky, depending on how you look at it—ones.

Standing in the mirror, I stare at myself in one of

my favourite fitted dresses and try to imagine what I might look like in a few months' time if I continue with this pregnancy. I always thought that, if I ever got pregnant, it would be when I was in a stable relationship, married even, and that it would be planned. I've always ensured I've stayed on top of my birth control to stop any unwanted surprises, but now it's here I don't really know what to think. Is it an unwanted surprise, or is it just one of those things that's meant to be? Is it a sign that Trey really could be the one and that we're destined for a life together? Is this the universe pushing us closer and making me pull my head out of my arse and ensuring that I accept how I really feel about him?

I rub my hand down over my flat stomach, thinking about how it might feel to have another person growing inside me. A part of me—a part of Trey.

My heart tumbles again. I need to tell him as soon as possible. I consider phoning him and arranging for us to have dinner here so I can do it in private, but I remember the excitement that glittered in his eyes as he told me about his favourite restaurant.

It'll be fine, I tell myself. *He'll totally accept it.*

Grabbing my phone to check the time, I find a voicemail from him. Quickly swiping the screen, I put it on speaker. It doesn't matter how many times I hear his deep voice, it still affects me like it did that first time he whispered in my ear at The Avenue all those weeks ago.

"Hey, sweetheart. I'm so sorry, I'm stuck in traffic. I've organised for a taxi to come and pick you up. I'll meet you at the restaurant. See you soon."

My stomach drops, knowing that I'm going to have to wait even longer to see him. I need to get the words out that have been taunting me since the moment I revealed the result on that little white stick. The more time I have, the more chance there is that I'll manage to talk myself out of telling him, and that can't happen.

Pulling on a pair of court shoes, I head out of the building to find the taxi he promised.

The second I pull the main door open, I spot the black cab idling outside.

"Erica?" he asks as I walk towards him.

"Yes."

I jump in the back and try to prepare for what tonight's going to bring. My stomach churns with nerves and I feel sicker than I have all day.

By the time the taxi pulls up outside the fancy restaurant, I'm a mess. My hands are trembling, my palms are sweating, and I can barely swallow, my mouth is so dry.

It'll be fine. It'll be fine, I chant as I walk inside and speak to the maître de.

He smiles warmly when I say Trey's name, and he tells me to follow to his favourite table.

I lower myself in the seat when he pulls it out and order myself a lime and soda to sip while I wait.

He's back within seconds and leaves me with the menus to browse. I flick it open but I don't see any of the words; they all just blur into a mix of letters and numbers as what I need to say to Trey runs around my head.

I'm totally lost in my own thoughts and it's not until the chair opposite me is pulled out and a body drops down onto it that I realise I have company.

Looking up, my brows draw together, a deep line forming between them as I stare at a woman. She looks kind of average and most definitely isn't dressed for this place, which confuses me even more.

"Hello," she says with the fakest smile I think I've ever seen.

"Uh...hi?"

"I know you're not expecting me." My eyes narrow as I try to figure out what she's saying. "I'm Sarah, Trey's wife. I thought it was time we met."

Erica and Trey's story continues in DEMANDING REDEMPTION.

ONE CLICK NOW

Have you read the first three books in the Forbidden series?
If not, you need to meet Lauren and Ben properly.
DOWNLOAD FALLING FOR THE FORBIDDEN NOW

ACKNOWLEDGMENTS

When I first embarked on this series, I had no idea that Erica was going to appear, but not long after writing her spunky office girl character, I knew that she had a story to tell. It's safe to say that she threw all my plans out of the window and started to tell me her story instead. And I'm so glad she did, because I love her. I love her hard outer shell that gives the impression that no one can touch her but, in reality, she's craving love and a happily ever after like everyone else. Much like Trey, really. How hot is he? I was really worried about the man who was going to follow on from Ben because he owns such a huge part of my heart, but Trey...I'm pretty sure he rose to the challenge with his dominance and sexy demands. Although he's got his work cut out for him after what's just happened. I'm excited to find out how he deals with it and wins his girl back.

A huge thank you once again to Michelle for being there every step of the way with this book. I couldn't do this without our daily chats, whether it be over tea and cake while the monsters play or over the phone. By the time this book releases it will be five years since we met. That day, neither of us knew it but our lives were about to change forever. Because of meeting you, I've done things I never ever thought I would, my life has changed in so many ways, and I know the woman who made it happen would be up there smiling down on us now, knowing she had a hand in it.

Deanna, Susanne and Tracy, thank you so much for picking up Erica and Trey's story the second it dropped on to your Kindles and your kind—and not so kind—messages about it. I appreciated every bit of your feedback more than you know, so thank you.

My long suffering editor, Evelyn. Thank you once again for taking my mess of words and commas and turning it into something readable! I could not do this without you.

Huge thank you to Paige who agreed to proofread this around her wedding. Massive congratulations and thank you so much for squeezing me in.

Thank you so much Samantha, who made the somewhat silly decision to help PA for me earlier in the summer. I am the world's worst control freak (sorry for not mentioning that sooner) but you've made my life so much easier and I can't thank you enough for all the time you've put into helping me find more time to write.

I've got so much heading your way—get those Kindles charged, you're going to need them!

Until next time,

Tracy xo

ABOUT THE AUTHOR

Tracy Lorraine is a *USA Today* and *Wall Street Journal* bestselling new adult and contemporary romance author. Tracy has recently turned thirty and lives in a cute Cotswold village in England with her husband, baby girl and lovable but slightly crazy dog. Having always been a bookaholic with her head stuck in her Kindle, Tracy decided to try her hand at a story idea she dreamt up and hasn't looked back since.

Be the first to find out about new releases and offers. Sign up to my newsletter here.

If you want to know what I'm up to and see teasers and snippets of what I'm working on, then you need to be in my Facebook group. Join Tracy's Angels here.

Keep up to date with Tracy's books at
www.tracylorraine.com

<u>Falling Series</u>

<u>Falling for Ryan: Part One</u> #1

<u>Falling for Ryan: Part Two</u> #2

<u>Falling for Jax</u> #3

<u>Falling for Daniel</u> (A Falling Series Novella)

<u>Falling for Ruben</u> #4

<u>Falling for Fin</u> #5

<u>Falling for Lucas</u> #6

<u>Falling for Caleb</u> #7

<u>Falling for Declan</u> #8

<u>Falling For Liam</u> #9

<u>Forbidden Series</u>

<u>Falling for the Forbidden</u> #1

<u>Losing the Forbidden</u> #2

<u>Fighting for the Forbidden</u> #3

<u>Craving Redemption</u> #4

<u>Demanding Redemption</u> #5

<u>Avoiding Temptation</u> #6

<u>Chasing Temptation</u> #7

<u>Rebel Ink Series</u>

<u>Hate You</u> #1

<u>Trick You</u> #2

<u>Defy You</u> #3

<u>Play You</u> #4

<u>Inked</u> (A Rebel Ink/Driven Crossover)

<u>Rosewood High Series</u>

<u>Thorn</u> #1

<u>Paine</u> #2

<u>Savage</u> #3

<u>Fierce</u> #4

<u>Hunter</u> #5

Faze (#6 Prequel)

<u>Fury</u> #6

<u>Legend</u> #7

<u>Maddison Kings University Series</u>

<u>TMYM: Prequel</u>

<u>TRYS</u> #1

<u>TDYW</u> #2

<u>TBYS</u> #3

<u>TVYC</u> #4

<u>TDYD</u> #5.

<u>TDYR</u> #6

<u>TRYD</u> #7

Knight's Ridge Empire Series

<u>Wicked Summer Knight</u>: Prequel (Stella & Seb)

<u>Wicked Knight</u> #1 (Stella & Seb)

<u>Wicked Princess</u> #2 (Stella & Seb)

<u>Wicked Empire</u> #3 (Stella & Seb)

<u>Deviant Knight</u> #4 (Emmie & Theo)

<u>Deviant Princess</u> #5 (Emmie & Theo

<u>Deviant Reign</u> #6 (Emmie & Theo)

<u>One Reckless Knight</u> (Jodie & Toby)

<u>Reckless Knight</u> #7 (Jodie & Toby)

<u>Reckless Princess</u> #8 (Jodie & Toby)

<u>Reckless Dynasty</u> #9 (Jodie & Toby)

<u>Dark Halloween Knight</u> (Calli & Batman)

<u>Dark Knight</u> #10 (Calli & Batman)

<u>Dark Princess</u> #11 (Calli & Batman)

Dark Legacy #12 (Calli & Batman)

Corrupt Valentine Knight (Nico & Siren)

<u>Ruined Series</u>

<u>Ruined Plans</u> #1

<u>Ruined by Lies</u> #2

<u>Ruined Promises</u> #3

<u>Never Forget Series</u>

<u>Never Forget Him</u> #1

<u>Never Forget Us</u> #2

<u>Everywhere & Nowhere</u> #3

<u>Chasing Series</u>

<u>Chasing Logan</u>

<u>The Cocktail Girls</u>

<u>His Manhattan</u>

<u>Her Kensington</u>

FALLING FOR THE FORBIDDEN
SNEAK PEEK
CHAPTER ONE

Falling down on my bed, I blow out a long breath and tell myself that everything will be okay.

I had plans for this summer—a few weeks of fun before uni starts. The girls and I had been looking at last-minute holiday deals, and we had tickets for a music festival...but then my dad swooped in, in that way that he does, and ruined everything.

I knew it was coming.

I just wasn't expecting it quite yet.

I'd hoped agreeing to study what he wanted me to and working for him was enough—apparently not.

I decided a few years ago that I wasn't going to move away to study. I mostly love my life in London, and I loved living with Mum. I'm not ashamed to admit that she's one of my best friends. It was only as I started looking at universities that my dad piped up and told me that I would be studying accountancy and finance at The London School of Economics. He'd done his research and decided it was the best place for me to learn my trade so I could enter the family business.

I just about managed to contain my laughter when he emphasised the word *family*.

I've no idea how long I lie on my bed trying to convince myself that moving into his house with his new wife and her son isn't the worst thing to ever happen to me, but eventually my stomach rumbling has me moving. I sit on the edge of the bed and take in all my half-unpacked boxes. A large sigh falls from my lips. If I don't find everything a home, maybe I won't have to stay. I know it's wishful thinking. This is it for me now.

Disappointment floods me as I make my way through the silent house. It's not that I was expecting a welcome party or anything, but someone being here would have been nice. Someone to help me carry everything up to my room would have been even nicer. Since Dad moved in with Jenny a few years ago, I've been told to treat this place like my home.

It will never be.

It's just a house, a show home, a shell in which I'm scared to touch anything for fear of making a mess. Home is a place with character, with mess from day-to-day living, with people who love and care for you.

My dad isn't a bad man, per se, but he's not exactly what you'd describe as a doting father. Everything he does is for his own gain—if it happens to help others in the process, that's just a bonus.

My step mum, Jenny, is lovely. She really is, but I can't help feeling like she's just a little bit...broken. She makes all the right comments and does all the right things. She's a great mum. But there's such sadness in her eyes.

The fridge is full, as usual. It's strange, because I've never witnessed anyone eating more than a slice of toast or an apple in this kitchen.

I fix myself a salad with the unopened packets of fruit and vegetables, but it doesn't really have the effect I needed it to have. Being here makes me feel kind of empty, and no amount of lettuce leaves is going to fill the void after moving out of the flat Mum and I shared for the past few years.

Rummaging through the cupboards, I can't help smiling when I find a stash of naughty stuff hiding at the back.

Pulling my hair back into a messy bun, I put my thoughts to the side and set about making something that will make me feel just a little bit better.

The sun's just about to set, casting an orange

glow throughout the kitchen. It almost makes it feel warm and inviting—almost. My mouth waters as I pour melted chocolate over the crushed biscuits and marshmallows I've managed not to eat already. Standing in only a vest and a small pair of hot pants, I decide to make myself a hot chocolate, grab a blanket, and enjoy my bowl of goodness out on the deck with a magazine. Chocolate makes everything that little bit better. If I eat enough, it might make me forget what this summer's actually going to be like for me.

I'm just waiting for the kettle to boil when a shiver runs down my spine. I'm sure it's just the size of the house that freaks me out. I've seen enough horror films to know there are plenty of hiding places in a place this big.

I'm still for a second, but when I don't hear anything, I continue with what I was doing. That is, until a deep rumbling voice has every nerve in my body on alert.

"Wow, step daddy sure is attracting the young ones these days." His voice is slurred, his anger palpable. It makes goosebumps prick my skin and a giant lump form in my throat. "You look too pure. Too innocent to be with that prick," he spits.

There's no love lost between my dad and my stepbrother, that's not news to me, but the viciousness of his voice right now makes me wonder what their relationship is really like. My dad might be many things, but he wouldn't cheat on Jenny—he loves her too much.

I can't remember the last time I saw him, but there's no way he can't know it's me. Who the hell else would be cooking in his kitchen? Deciding he's just trying to rile me up, I go to collect my stuff and get out of his way. Unfortunately, he seems to have other ideas.

His breath tickles up my neck moments before the heat of his body warms my back.

"You came here for the wrong man. I can put that right, though." The alcohol on his breath surrounds me. It's a reminder that there's a good chance he has no idea what he's doing right now.

The softness of his nose running up the length of my neck has tingles racing through my traitorous body. I don't realise he's smelling me until he blows out a long breath and the scent of alcohol hits me once again. I turn to leave, but his hands slam on the counter behind me and cage me in.

"Look at me," he demands.

"Let me go, Ben."

If he's surprised to discover it's me, he doesn't show it. If anything, his eyes shine with delight as he takes in every inch of my face before focusing on my lips. My stomach flips, knowing where his thoughts are.

Something passes over his face but it's gone too quickly to be able to identify. He pushes himself from the counter and away from me. No more words are said, but when he gets to the door, he looks back over his shoulder and runs his eyes over my body. They hold a warning I don't really understand.

Once he's disappeared from sight, I sag back against the counter. What the hell was that?

After putting half of the rocky road on a tray in the fridge, I forgo sitting outside and instead take my spoils to my room to hide. There's stuff everywhere in my room and, unlike the rest of this house, it makes me feel a little more relaxed.

Since the day Ben and I were introduced by our parents, we've not really had any kind of relationship. He's pretty much stayed out of my way and, in turn, I've done the same. It's not all that much of a task. When I'm here, he spends almost every minute somewhere else. When he's home, he's moody, arrogant, and generally a prick, so I'm more than happy to stay out of his way.

It's just a shame he's so damn pretty to look at. As the years have passed, he's only become more attractive, too. I've no idea if it's just his job or if he works out as well because every inch of him seems to be toned to perfection.

Jenny spends most of her time apologising for his attitude and trying to explain that he's got a lot going on. I'm yet to discover what that is. As far as I can tell, he seems to be your average twenty-year-old guy who'd rather be off his arse drunk or with a woman than spending time at home with his parents.

By the time I've dug my way to the bottom of the bowl, I feel pretty sick. There's still no sign of my dad or Jenny, but the music pounding from Ben's room across the hallway leaves no doubt as to what kind of mood he's in.

DOWNLOAD NOW to continue Lauren and Ben's story.